Tree Talk

TREE TALK

Ana Salote

Speaking Tree

First published in 2007 by Speaking Tree
10A Shrubbery Walk, Weston-Super-Mare
Somerset BA23 2JE

Distributed by Gardners Books, 1 Whittle Drive, Eastbourne,
East Sussex, BN23 6QH

All the characters in this book are fictitious and any resemblance to actual creatures, living or dead, is purely imaginary – except for the tree which is real.

British Library Cataloguing in Publication Data
A catalogue record for this book is available from the British Library.

ISBN 978-0-9553769-0-0

Typeset by Amolibros, Milverton, Somerset
This book production has been managed by Amolibros

Printed and bound by T J International Ltd, Padstow, Cornwall, UK

About the Author

Ana Salote is a tutor and environmental activist. She lives in Somerset and in books and wouldn't like to choose between them. *Tree Talk* is an environmental parable for all ages set against a background of oil wars and climate change. This book involves children in the most important questions facing the world today in a quirky and original way.

Contents

Foreword

This is a story for all human children, even if they consider themselves grown-ups. We are in a predicament of our own unknowing making, caused by our inability to connect with the animals and plants with whom we share this small planet. Ana takes us into the world of a small boy who does make a profound connection with a tree. This connection sparks a consciousness in plant life. The boy-tree link is the thread through this story, which is at times dark and funny, serious and sad. It is our story into the future as the crises of climate change and the end of the oil age unfold. The human weaknesses of greed and selfishness are countered with acts of love and caring. The calamities that result from the crises are met in the true British fashion of muddling through, reminding us that the collapse of societies and civilisations may happen in a graceful way.

The young boy, Charlie, is our hero. His understanding of the value of all living things is the key to our eventual second chance at a council of all beings. We are left with a sense that a rightful science, applied in humility, may repair and restore the damage unleashed by that misnamed creature Homo sapiens. There is hope but this is a story that does not shy away from the awfulness of what we face. I hope that many children will read this and get a glimpse of the wonder and awesomeness of life, that they will follow Charlie's example of loving life and treating it with deep respect.

I highly recommend this tale. If you ever thought that a tree can think then now you will know – go touch a tree.

Ian Roderick
Director, Schumacher Institute for Sustainable Systems

1

The Treehouse

In a garden you have to get on with your neighbours; you can't pack up and move away. Growing up, there were times when I wanted to fight for light and air and water, when it was my instinct to lean over and choke the other guy or wrap my roots around his. But I've learned a few things since then. First, if you go too far the gardener might come along and chop you back; second, you've got to live with yourself; and third, you wouldn't really want to overrun the whole garden, would you; where's the interest in that?

Our garden is mostly a place of harmony. Eva, our gardener, knows when to interfere and when to let us be.

In many ways our garden is unusual. The house is part of a grand Victorian terrace called Overvale Mansions. There are five houses standing together like great stone ships facing out to sea. The gardens slope gently at first and then drop steeply down the hillside.

Eva lets the steep part of her garden run wild. It starts as an orchard but soon becomes a wilderness. Eva's boy, Charlie, calls it the Jungle.

We've only to look over the fences to realise how lucky we are. Graham, next door, is hopeless. His garden is a space for fixing bikes. He has a cracked patio, scrubby, tyre-marked grass, and a few valiant daffs in his borders. Even worse, to my mind, is the garden which borders the far end of the Jungle. The lawn's like a carpet; the flowers look plastic; the shrubs are cut into rigid shapes. It's a dead garden: no birds, no insects, no moss, no moulds, not even the memory of a weed. It belongs to the Sperrins.

In my early days I knew little of humans, though I was aware of our gardener. A lot of plants, when they're being fed and watered, think of it as a kind of surprise weather. Only the sensitive ones, like myself, sense the gardener at the end of the hose. Over the years I got more interested in the gardener. I noticed she had a little helper: one who ate soil, made potions and stirred things with sticks, and I began to look forward to him coming out to play. Even then I felt drawn to Charlie.

The day of my awakening came when I was sixty-two rings wide. A pleasant spring breeze ruffled my leaves. A circle of humans surrounded my trunk.

Now you must understand that until that day I was just like all the other plants. I lived in a sort of green vapour, not quite sure where I ended and the rest of the world began. I took a passing interest in birds and bugs, but my main concern was the weather; and if you were to put yourself in my place for just a minute you'd know why. Imagine living your whole life standing outside, without clothes, in the same spot; you only get a drink when it rains, and the sun feeds you. Wouldn't you be obsessed with the weather? Anyway that was my world: I enjoyed light, but I didn't see as you see; I felt vibrations, but I didn't hear as you hear.

It's hard for me now to remember what it was like. I felt humans as different types of energy. On that day I saw the human energy around my trunk as a patchy spray of orange; a short strong column of violet, which I recognized as Eva; and a little ball of pure white energy, which I also knew well. The white ball rolled over to me. I felt a small warm spot against my bark. This, it turned out, was Charlie's hand.

There I stood, no more than mildly curious about the bobbing glowballs around me, when I was rocked from roots to shoots. A wave of light washed through me; I felt Charlie with his hand joined to me like an extra branch and I knew the world as Charlie knew it. I could see! The energy blobs had forms and faces beyond imagination. I watched Charlie's dad, Pete, stacking planks of wood around my trunk; I saw Eva shielding her eyes—eyes, what astonishing things—and peering up into my branches, and Charlie's sketches spread on the ground around me. Charlie was standing back from me, open-mouthed with his arms hanging loose and my own green light dappling his skin. He backed away from me without taking his eyes off my branches and tugged at Eva's sleeve.

'Mum.'

'Just a minute.'

'Mum.'

'What?'

'The tree. I know how it feels.'

'What, funny boy?' she said laughing.

'I really, really know how it feels.'

'Well ask it if it minds me knocking some nails in it,' drawled Pete.

'All right,' and Charlie put his hand on my trunk and asked: did I mind if they built a treehouse in my branches? It would be like a bird's nest but for humans. His dad was clever; he would try not to use too many nails. I told Charlie—by that I mean my feelings somehow spilled into Charlie's head—that I didn't mind, but it was just shock talking: a human was conversing with me and I was answering.

'The tree said it doesn't mind,' said Charlie.

Eva laughed again. Charlie knew it was pointless trying to explain, and quietly stood aside, though his eyes were sparking with discovery. We made a pact of secrecy right there.

Pete put a ladder up against me and climbed in among my branches. I was taken aback, never having had anything larger than a cat climb into me. He went back down, pulled out some nasty-looking tools and went to work on the planks of wood. I started to get worried then. The sound of that saw so close was freezing my sap, but Charlie stood by, patting my trunk; the edges of our minds were still touching and I calmed down.

It took a few days to finish the treehouse. Most of it was done with rope and pegs and Charlie helped Eva to weave the walls so that it looked like a giant bird's nest. This was all made easier, Eva said, because I was very tall and sturdy for a mountain ash. She thought I must be some unknown hybrid.

There was a chain ladder, which Charlie could pull up if he didn't want to be disturbed, and a thick piece of rope that hung down as an emergency exit.

The treehouse was almost finished when Charlie stopped his excited jigging and stared up at his bedroom window. A smile of inspiration spread over his face. He ran to Pete, who was lounging on the grass with a cup of tea, and, moving Pete's long hair to one side, whispered in his ear.

'That's crazy,' Pete laughed.

'Oh can you try, please? It will be so great. Please.'

'Your ma won't like it.'

Next morning Charlie went off to school and Eva left for work. Pete paced up and down, idly tuning his guitar. Then he laughed out loud, played a few wild chords, and disappeared. I relaxed into a green trance, turning minutely so that each leaf followed the sun's drift and caught its light squarely. The sun, the sun; I joined the rest of the garden in its chant. Suddenly a crashing hole appeared under Charlie's bedroom window. Stones bounced off my trunk and settled around my roots. A man's face looked through the hole with Pete at his shoulder. I stared back at them.

By the end of the day I was joined to the house.

The two men had built a hatch, like a giant cat flap, under Charlie's window. From this a chute led directly into the treehouse.

Eva and Charlie arrived home together. Eva stood on the lawn with her hand over her mouth while Charlie hung round Pete's waist saying, 'Thank you, thank you, thank you,' before flying upstairs. Soon he came bursting out of the chute into the treehouse. For the next hour a hot, excited boy went whirling through the house and down the chute, appearing head first, then feet first, on his back and on his belly. He tried to climb back up the chute but couldn't do it until Pete fixed some handles to the sides.

Charlie was too busy to hear Eva and Pete arguing in the kitchen. It was something about money, and why didn't Pete get a job instead of demolishing the house; nothing of interest really. I went back to watching Charlie.

You might imagine that I would object to all this interference, but the opposite is true. My trunk had split into a natural cup as though waiting for this very structure, and five strong branches curved out from it like a protective hand. When the treehouse was finished it felt as though a gap had been filled. I was complete.

2

Growing

Then began the golden days, the last days.

In the beginning I found it tiring to stay tuned to the human way of seeing things. There was far too much to take in. I often sank back into my own green world, but that wasn't enough for me any more. I had developed a burning curiosity about all things human.

Soon I couldn't wait for Charlie to come out each day, and he was just as curious about me. We communicated directly mind to mind, and day after day we questioned each other, what it was to be human, what it was to be tree.

I asked Charlie, 'Where in your body do you feel you are?'

He closed his eyes and seemed to be checking out bits of his body.

'I'm not there, not there. I'm not there. I'm there. I'm in my forehead.

'So what does it feel like to be a tree?' Charlie asked.

'Go sit on the grass down there and I'll show you.'

I dropped back into what I call my green state and let Charlie in. He stood up and opened his arms wide and raised his face to the sun.

'I feel like a giant,' he laughed, 'and the light, the sunlight's pouring energy into me; it's so satisfying. I want to stretch up and meet the sun. And my feet, all my toes are growing, ooh h-hoo, burrowing through the ground. I'm all cold at the bottom and warm on top, and I feel joined up with everything.'

It was my turn again. 'What are eyes for?'

'I sense light and colour with them. Do you know that you were probably the first thing I ever saw?'

'How could that be?'

'I was born just there under the window.'

'And you were the first thing I ever saw,' I said, 'properly I mean.' We marvelled quietly for a minute.

'There's something more about eyes,' I said, looking into Charlie's, which were full of fun and wonder, whitish-green with dancing bird's egg speckles.

'Your eyes are just below the place where *you* are, and you shed your light through them, so your eyes show who you really are.'

'If you say so, Ash.'

'I knew there was something special about eyes.'

Besides Charlie, I had another teacher. I had grown some branches across the lounge windows so that I could watch Eva and Charlie before the curtains were drawn. Charlie would be sprawled on the rug. Eva would be sorting through paperwork or reading. Sometimes they'd look up at a square of light in the corner and sometimes they'd sit together on the sofa and just stare at this coloured light with moving patterns in it. So I tried staring at it too. Gradually I learned to see that the moving patterns were pictures, like the real world but smaller and flatter, and I learned that by watching this square I could find out much more about humans than I could ever know by standing in a garden.

I watched and watched and learned about things that happened long ago and far away; about other plants and animals and the sea and planets; things I'd felt in my green days but never seen and things that amazed me. My favourite programmes were the soaps, because they put together two things which fascinated me: stories and human behaviour, *Brooke Farm* is the best of the soaps because it has the most weather in it.

But the real secret of humans I discovered by accident. It's obvious that human bodies aren't stuck in one place like trees, but neither are their minds. They go back. They go forward. And they go some place else. Up? Or down? Whatever, it was a direction my mind didn't have. Now I can do some of these tricks. Back is my weather memory; forward is my weather instinct. I got my first clue to the other direction as I listened to Charlie one day.

He was lying in the grass with his magnifying glass watching the beetles scurrying among the roots when he began talking to himself:

'Now the challenger beetle in his great armoured coat stalks the deserted streets of the city, hunting down the copperhead. The way is strewn with obstacles but he knows them not. Under, over, boulders, thatch; the copperhead wanders unaware, rubs his feet together in the sun, lazily twirls his antennae. The challenger storms through the grass; big as a house; great swivelling eyes precede him. A cloud passes over the sun; the copperhead bows; his hour has come. But what is this? He is taken up and away, saved by a hair's breadth,' and Charlie whisked the little beetle away on a lollipop stick.

'What was all that about?' I asked.

Charlie explained about stories. It seems that while plants think moment by moment; humans think in chains, and chains are stories. And get this, the stories don't have to be real.

'So,' I said, 'you can have things in your mind that never happened?'

'Yes.'

'In that case, you can have whatever you like in your mind!'

'Yes—it's called imagination.'

I felt brambles clearing, paths opening into space. The freedom.

'Careful though, Ash; it also means you can have things you don't want in your mind.'

'And what's that called.'

'Worry.'

Something I would come to know well, but not then. Those first weeks of our friendship were the best and the most exciting days of my life. Then something happened which made Charlie close his mind to me.

I had noticed something odd about Eva and Pete. When they were together their auras shrank and grew duller; only when Charlie came into the room did they start to glow again. One morning, when Charlie was at school, I heard muffled shouting from the front rooms, the ones I can't see into. This went on for some time; then I heard thumping on the stairs, more shouting, a stunning door slam, then a deeper quiet filled with a feeling of sadness and something broken.

Out in the garden, life went on; birds sang and insects trekked about as usual. At school, I knew that Charlie would be playing or working cheerfully, and for once I didn't wish him home.

Charlie told me how the idea of the treehouse had always been with him. At nursery he had looked around the table at other children's drawings of houses with smoky chimneys and spiky suns, sometimes with a tree to one side. Then he had scrabbled in the box of fat crayons and started to draw his own idea of home. Charlie drew his house *in* the tree. The teacher couldn't work out what it was to begin with. As he got older the drawings got better and more detailed, and he regularly presented them to his dad asking when, when will you build me a treehouse? The treehouse, it turned out, was a goodbye gift.

After his dad left, Charlie would come up and lie on his back on the platform staring up into my leaves which went up and up in green steps, up into the blue; and I couldn't tell what he was thinking, only that he wasn't happy.

I heard Eva talking to her friend Brigid in the kitchen.

'I'm okay, it's Charlie I'm worried about. He's barely spoken for two weeks, just sits up in that treehouse, moping.'

'Distract him—treat him to something nice,' was Brigid's advice.

So Eva bought him toys. He piled them in his room, still boxed, and eventually told her, 'Mum, you don't have to, I'm all right.'

Looking into him, I knew that things were growing and rearranging inside him and that took time. Still I thought Brigid's advice was good so I tried a distraction of my own.

One of the things that humans do is give names to things. I still don't know why they do this. Things which seem unimportant, like bits of plastic with wires sticking out, have complicated names like digital transponder unit, whereas very important and complicated things like the weather have a few simple names: rain, sun, wind. I thought I would put this right. I let Charlie understand the millions of different weathers that plants know of and I started to name them all for him. At first he looked listless and uninterested.

'Take the weather today. It's galooshty. Humans call it windy. He-llo, last weekend they also called windy, and the Tuesday before that—all different if you think back. Now today the trees look lively and the grass is flattened. There are long, low gusts with a billowing somewhere beyond, like someone's shaking out a wet sheet in the sky.'

Charlie had cocked his head towards me; at last he was listening.

'April 3rd '93 was very similar,' I said, matching tree-time to the human calendar, as I had learned to do.

'How'd you know that?' he said.

'I keep the story of the weather in the rings inside my trunk,' I said. 'I often run back through them, especially in winter, and dwell on fine spells.'

'Wow—' the little scientist in him was now fully awake and curious, '—so, can you tell me what the weather was like on the day I was born?'

'Let me see. Yes, aaah, of all weathers, the most perfect. Early autumn, placid, unstirring, golden. You may have noticed that there are only three or four days a year when no human finds fault with the weather. Your birthday was such a day.'

'Good, I'll name that weather goldumbra.'

'Yes, goldumbra,' and as I said it, another memory came to me, one I had put aside on the edges of the weather. I remembered white light coming into being right there under the window, and out of that light, eyes of astonishment looking straight at me.

And so we went on, going back through my rings. I showed him the best and worst of days and lots in between and we named them all: greezy, sottoverdi, blanckwick, munglub; and so on.

Charlie sucked it all in with his head on one side. I could feel his brain whirring and processing until he had reached an understanding that only plants seem to possess: what could be more important than weather? It nursed life itself.

He sat quietly then, cross-legged on his high perch looking out across the canopy of the Jungle, out towards the grey line of the sea. It pleased me to see him so impressed by knowledge that we plants take for granted.

'So it's all connected,' he said, 'every breath I take, every breath you take, Ash, it all adds up to...' and then he wrapped his arms tightly around himself and I swear he looked as though a storm was swirling around him, pulling at his face, slanting his eyes, tearing at his clothes. It was a windy day, but not that windy. As the mini-tempest passed he stood unsteadily and shading his eyes looked slowly over the whole sky and then at the Jungle tree by tree.

'It can't be,' he breathed. 'That is...boggling. Phew!' He shook his head.

Charlie had put plant instinct together with human imagination and he had come up with something greater than both. At the time it was beyond my grasp. Now I know, I think only a child could have faced what he saw, and then said what he said so matter-of-factly.

'There's work to be done, Ash,' and he slid down the rope, muttering, 'but where do I start?'

'Windy tonight,' said Eva, looking up from her book.

'It's galooshty with a bite in it,' Charlie replied with a new spark in his eyes.

Eva smiled, thinking, no doubt, that the old Charlie was back. I wanted to tell her that my distraction had worked much better than I'd intended.

3

Wilfred

As I said, I quickly became a fan of humans. I found them endlessly interesting, complex and clever; but not everyone feels that way.

One evening, as I practised some human sayings, I was distracted by scrabbling and sniffing around my roots. I looked down to see a large rat stuffing his cheeks with my berries.

In my first life as I think of it, in my dreamy, greeny days, I'd sensed Wilfred as a busy, deep red energy. I was aware that he was different to the other animals—there was more going on in him, and when I first saw him properly he looked different too. He was bigger and paler than the other rats. His fur was a mixture of brown and white, making him look aged, but his eyes were sharp and canny.

He spun round in surprise.

'Well I'm blowed,' he said, looking up into my branches, 'this is a first; how did you come by it?'

‘By what?’ I asked, as much surprised as he was.

‘Gnosis,’ he said, ‘I’ve never known a tree with it.’

And we fell to talking and that was the start of our friendship. Gnosis, he explained, was this extra way of seeing things that I’d got from Charlie. He’d never heard of it passing from humans in this way, and he lifted up on his legs and twitched and quivered in fascination. He himself had got it from eating a fungus, something his mother had told him never to go near or he’d never be happy again. But, being the nosiest rat born, he had had a nibble and found his skull split ear to ear with this knowing. I knew just how he felt of course. My berries, he told me, had similar effects.

‘I wonder, is it possible that your own dryad absorbed the essence of your berries, thus predisposing you to the boy’s vibrations?’

‘Dryad?’

‘Spirit. Tree spirit. A purely technical point, but interesting.’

When he says things like that I realise just how much I have to learn. We talked long into that night, comparing notes about our experiences. While Wilfred didn’t know of any plants with gnosis he knew of many animals. Most had got it in the same way as himself, but he also knew of a family of magpies where it passed down through the generations. One ancient magpie was very skilled at precognosis—reading the future from natural signs. These few hundred animals formed a council, which met every three years to discuss, among other things, the human problem.

Wilfred said that getting my gnosis directly from a human was a bad thing: it made me see them in a good light, and he set out to educate me properly.

He gave me the first of his lectures then, one that I've since heard many times. To my mind his hatred of humans isn't quite rational. They make him shudder. They're vermin, he says. What are vermin I says? Vermin, he says, are dirty; they spread disease, feed on waste and breed uncontrollably.'

'On the other branch,' I said, 'they can be very kind. My gardener takes good care of me, and Charlie...'

'Ash, you're so domesticated,' Wilfred interrupted—he's not a good listener, 'you've heard your mates out in the woods and meadows, and in the hedgerows.'

Actually, for a long while, I hadn't been listening.

'There's been so much death out there. Who gave the humans the right to decide who's a weed and who's not? They say they're doing it for the crops but even the crops have started to complain. They don't like being sprayed and regimented, there's no variety any more, they're forced to grow quick and exhausted, only the big ones get to breed. At first they thought: great, no caterpillars, no aphids munching on us; then they noticed the silence: no bustle, no visitors, everybody the same size and shape, and they sunk into this quiet depression. They used to feel part of a bigger picture where everybody gets a piece of the action; not any more, the vermin want all the benefits for themselves.'

He was right about the 'weeds', and so my doubts began.

'If only those plants could be taught to think like you,' he went on, 'then they could do something about it. Then what a power we would be, flora and fauna, together against the vermin.' He bared his yellow teeth and his eyes flashed with fervour.

It was then that I learned how to lie, or rather how to hide parts of my mind. I thought it best if I didn't worry Charlie with Wilfred's plotting. Already I was being torn between them. I started keeping score. Were humans mostly good, or were they vermin? I imagined notches on my trunk like this: Human IIIII Vermin I. It amused me but I never really doubted that Wilfred was wrong.

One night Wilfred came early, puffed up and gleeful with his tidings. But I already knew. I had seen it on TV.

We were watching the news before *Brooke Farm*, when Eva grabbed the remote, turned the sound up and sat forward. I wouldn't have paid attention normally but she looked so worried that I tried to understand what was going on. There was stuff about men in suits and men in headdresses who didn't agree about this and that. Then men all dressed the same made things explode and dropped things out of aeroplanes and made things burn and trees burn and people burn. It was a relief when the weather came on, as this was easy to understand.

Human weather forecasts are embarrassing. They're so simple and often wrong. But even the weather forecast was different that day. They were saying things about icecaps melting; there were pictures of somewhere cold and far away, and there was ice falling into the sea, not little chunks but walls of it, miles wide, breaking off and melting into the blue-black water. The weather, they said, was going to change quickly and dramatically, and that also had something to do with oil.

I didn't understand it, but Wilfred was more than happy to explain:

'The oil-agers,' he said, 'have come to the end of their age. The oil would have lasted them a while longer but they had to start fighting over it; now what's left of it is burning; half the planet is on fire. It was bound to happen. Let's hope they all kill each other quickly and let the planet heal. Maybe a few stragglers will survive, like the old stone-agers. Ah, the stone-agers; they were no bother; I got along with them just fine. Do you know why? They didn't get above themselves. It started to go wrong when they gave themselves that name: Homo sapiens. It means wise man. How vain, how pompous, how deluded! Homo selfish idiot is more accurate.'

'Or Verman,' I said.

'Clever,' he said, 'vermin, verman. Why didn't I think of that one? Yes, noble Rattus sapiens battles plague of vermanity. That's the real truth.'

I hadn't meant to go along with him like that, but his character is old and strong, while mine is new and suggestible. He sneaks into my mind and takes over. 'So,' I said, after thinking some more, 'the end of the Oil Age, what does it mean?'

'A lot of the bad things are going,' said Wilfred, 'cars first. Just watch; enjoy watching them cling to their dying age.'

So I watched and he was right. The traffic hum that I was born into faded right away. The lights that hid the stars every night went out at midnight. A few months later they were out by ten o'clock. These were the nice things.

Not so good were the days when the power was cut off in the middle of a soap; but for the humans, Wilfred said, there were harder times to come, and he scurried off chanting to himself: 'Rattus sapiens, Rattus sapiens shall inherit the earth.'

As usual, there was nothing I could do but watch.

4

The Task Begins

Humans, as far as I can tell, don't usually begin their life's work at the age of ten. Charlie did.

For his birthday he asked for a particular gift. It was a goldumbra afternoon and the party had spilled out into the garden. Since morning, Charlie had been in a strange mood. He had woken excited, thumped downstairs for the post, then turned quiet. At the party there was something brittle about him. He opened presents and thanked his friends politely. I couldn't read his thoughts and every now and again I saw him staring vacantly into the distance.

Eva appeared with a heavy rainbow-wrapped cube on top of which was a big silver ten on a spring. His friends oohed and aahed. 'Bet it's a robot,' someone whispered. Charlie laid the ten to one side and carefully unpicked the tape.

'Rip it!' George urged him.

Charlie opened out the paper and brushed his hand

over the cover of Birtwhistle's *Complete Botany of British Plants* in three volumes. I watched his face carefully and I saw that his eyes glowed.

'Flower books,' said Dan.

'They're nice,' said Izzy, but her nose was wrinkled.

George snatched at a plastic toy. 'Let's have a go with this then. Ugh, there's an earwig on it. I hate earwigs,' he said and stabbed the creature through the head with a biro.

The earwig, with its head pinned to the picnic table, waved its body helplessly. Charlie froze. He bent forward as though winded, then reached over and took the pen out of George's hand.

'You *don't* just break an animal like a toy,' Charlie said quietly.

George shrugged. 'Sor-ree, it's an earwig, not an elephant.'

'The earwig doesn't know that,' said Conal, rather wisely I thought.

The party was dampened until Eva came out again, this time carrying a green cake streaming ten spots of light. In the middle of the cake sprouted a tree with red berries: me I guessed, with a tickle of satisfaction.

'Why has it got skunks on it?' George whispered.

'They're badgers, stupid,' said Conal.

Happy Birthday was sung in three different keys with a staggered ending.

'Make a wish,' said Eva.

'Mmm, I've got more than one,' said Charlie twisting his hands.

'Well make two then; I think it's allowed.'

'Three actually.'

'What do you think?' Eva asked the party. 'Do we let him have three?'

'I made three once; none of them came true though,' said Jade.

Charlie screwed up his eyes and his lips moved silently through three wishes.

I heard his wishes but since birthday wishes are secret I can't tell you what they were. The first wish was no surprise, the second wish was made with such power that his aura crackled, the third wish staggered me; it was on a scale I couldn't have guessed at.

He had, when he opened his eyes, the look of a storm-blasted sapling. I followed his eyes to the earwig which got up, clicked its head back into place and slipped out of sight. A few minutes later, Graham, from next door, appeared with an envelope. It was for Charlie and had gone to the wrong address. Charlie ripped it open and beamed.

'Dad's coming over in two weeks,' he said and skipped around the garden.

Two out of three, I thought.

I don't think I'm giving anything away if I say that the third wish had something to do with our garden. Our humble little garden; how could it be so important, so very important? Surely it was just a child's fantasy? But what a fantasy.

The very next day Charlie began working on his third wish. Armed with Birtwhistle's *Botany* he told me only that he was going to identify every plant in the garden from the smallest grass to the biggest tree.

'Why?' I said.

'I need to be ready,' he said.

'What for?' I called, but he was already off down the garden with his books and pens and magnifying glass.

Hours later he came back and showed me his drawings.

'They are very good,' I said, 'but it's not like that really.'

'What do you mean?'

'A plant doesn't live on its own like that. You need to learn how to watch. It's a tree thing; it comes from being stuck in one place. Come and watch my branch for five minutes and you'll see what I mean.'

'Wow, Ash,' he said, 'you're Insect City,' and we looked at my lodgers together: at small wings paned like glass and shot with rainbows, at tiny hairs and scales and sculpted heads.

Charlie practised watching every day after that. He got better and better at it, so that sometimes the plants forgot that he wasn't just one of them. He added notes to his drawings about which insects preferred which plants, which plants grew together and how the weather acted like a conductor, telling them when to bud, flower and fruit.

'That's better,' I said, 'now you're getting the whole picture. That's the most important thing. Don't forget that.'

Charlie looked at me with his head on one side, and we had a sort of joint premonition. 'No, I won't forget that,' he said.

He also drew a scale plan of the garden marked into squares. The squares were named after features; like moss chair, fungus face, big beetle log. Each plant was given a number and its locations marked on the plan.

The days were growing shorter but he still came out in all weather and drew until dusk, then he would come up to the treehouse, look up the plants in the fat volumes and learn all the Latin names.

'*Sorbus aucuparia*, that's your posh name,' he told me, reading from Birtwhistle, 'only thing is you're four times as big as you should be. I've got a theory about that.'

'Yes?'

'Well your memory is in your rings, and you have more memory than other trees, so you're bigger. You're upgraded like a computer. Or maybe your seeds dropped in from space. Anyway, it says here you're also known as Rowan, Witch-wood, Witchen and Quickbeam. Quick comes from Anglo-Saxon cwic—oh wow, guess what cwic means.'

'I don't know.'

'Alive!' and he lay on his back giggling.

I like it when he does that. At other times, as he drew, he looked serious, even sad.

'What is it?' I asked.

'It's starting,' he said. 'Beech is suffering most, but there are others. I should start the seed collection.'

'What are you talking about?'

'Don't bother yet, it could be just a blip,' and he pulled himself up the chute to his room where I watched him gluing matchboxes together and slotting them into shoeboxes. Every day he put seeds in the boxes and labelled them neatly.

I was pleased to be included. He rescued the last of my berries, which were already shrivelled and brown, squashed them, and picked out the seeds. A single seed, no more than a brown fleck, lay on the palm of his hand.

'That's the most amazing thing. You grew out of one of these.'

I didn't think it was amazing. It's what trees have always done. Charlie picked up my thoughts.

'All the instructions for making you are in this speck.'

I was still unimpressed, but I did like how Charlie put my seeds in their own special box with the ends coloured red. He put it next to a picture of his dad. I heard him tell Conal that those were the things he would take if the house burned down.

A few days later Charlie lay on his bed with a letter. Pete wasn't coming. Someone had broken into his flat and nicked his guitar, phone and wallet. He had asked Eva to lend him money till his next gig.

'Want to talk?' I asked Charlie.

He shook his head and started digging through the layers of rubbish, as Eva calls it, on his bedroom floor. Charlie says it's not rubbish, it's all useful, and he knows where everything is. He flung things aside like a rabbit digs up earth. A year-old banana skin flew past me. Finally he rummaged in a box of pictures and cuttings under his bed. He came up from the fluff and dust with something in his hand.

'What's that?' I asked.

'It's a postcard for Dad, look, with a picture of a Strat—that's a guitar he likes.'

Charlie wrote:

> Dad,
>
> I am sorry you got robbed. I know you will come as soon as you can. I am doing a project about the garden. It is really interesting. So far I have found seventy-two different plants. Mum likes the drawings I have done. She has helped with colouring. When you come I will tell you what the project is really about.
>
> love Charlie

The next time I saw that guitar picture it was sticking out from a pile of bills on the table. Charlie was smearing Birtwhistle with toast butter as he read. Eva tutted and Charlie looked up.

'Sorry love, your card's come back. No forwarding address,' she said.

'So we don't know where he is?'

'I'm sorry.'

His eyes grew a little bit older. After that Charlie

worked even harder on the project. One day he clambered up breathlessly to tell me that he had found a plant not mentioned in Birtwhistle. He showed me his sketch and together we named it *Junglus slaterii*. No detail of the garden escaped him. He even described the dance of falling leaves: how some rock like swingboats, and others, like sycamore, swirl down stem first.

My own last leaf dropped, and so, for me, came darkness. Winter is my night, though I can see through Charlie's mind when he is near. But winter was shorter than ever. I felt like spring was shaking me awake just minutes after I'd fallen asleep. Very soon my buds were green enough to see the first catkins, and gnats dodging web skeins in the slanting light. With the surge of spring I cast around for a project of my own. I didn't have to look very far.

Holly was the first. She grows opposite me on the other side of the kitchen window and our roots are politely intertwined. The wakening didn't come to Holly in a flash as it did with me. Holly described it as echoes coming through a fog, and I was the source. She felt echoes and shadows of my thoughts for a long time, but she couldn't catch hold or make sense of them. As soon as I felt her budding mind groping towards mine, I started to teach her and she caught on very quickly.

First I taught her how to translate light and sound waves into humanish sight and hearing. She loved Lesson 3: Cause and Effect—a new look at weather. Lesson 6: Making Stories, took her a while to get.

In the past we plants had our stories: a sort of endless whispering about the weather, but nothing on the scale of human tales.

'Stories are just cause and effect with different leaves,' I told her, but it didn't really click until I showed her *Brooke Farm*.

Lesson 8, Understanding Humans Part 1, was hard work. I was trying for the umpteenth time to explain to Holly about beauty. Eva is an artist. She throws open a window to watch a special sunset, and murmurs things like:

'The artless art of it; the throwaway, heartbreaking signature of God up there,' and she laughs and puts her arm round Charlie who knows what she means and through him I'll feel a glimmer too. But explaining it to Holly was tricky.

'Beautiful things are things that humans like to look at, and it makes them feel good,' I said.

' Why?' she wanted to know.

'That's something I'm still looking into,' I said, 'just try to accept it for now.'

Charlie climbed the ladder. For once he listened to me when I told him to take a break; he was just a child after all. The grass cuttings, which Eva had heaped under the treehouse, steamed faintly in the sun, sweet with daisy heads and dandelion clippings. Charlie flopped backwards into it, he flopped forwards into it, he flew scissor-shaped, leapt knees tucked, somersaulted. He rolled around till he looked like some sort of mad grass boy. It was too distracting. I abandoned Beauty.

When he had exhausted every possible kind of leap, he went for a walk through the orchard; a hairy green animal he seemed. As he walked, he touched the trees alternately to one side and then the other. At the bottom of the Orchard, where two cherry trees form an arch into the Jungle, Charlie stopped with a hand on each bole.

'Whoah,' he said looking back over his shoulder with a big grin, then slowly scanning the whole garden. 'Can you feel that?' he asked. 'It's all prickling, it's all coming alive.'

It was true; along with its spring buds the whole garden was budding awareness.

It seemed that a sort of diluted gnosis had passed along my roots and from plant to plant.

Over the next few days the waking rolled down the garden reaching all the way to the edge of the Jungle. Flowers and leaves burst open in spontaneous surprise. The garden buzzed with questions and confusion. Remembering how awakening felt, I couldn't just leave them to it. I did my best to guide them.

Each plant came along at its own pace, but few were as quick as Holly. Most of them could only think for a small part of the day and some of them preferred not to do it at all. It didn't matter. In the end my influence showed in two things: they all loved Charlie and they were all addicted to stories—well okay, *Brooke Farm*.

The other plants couldn't talk to Charlie like I could, but they bonded with him anyway. That was why Eva's plan came as such a shock to all of us. I don't blame Eva though; after the oil wars, she was just trying to survive.

5

Garden for Sale

All the surprises in my life have come when I least expect them. If I had a better imagination perhaps I would be ready.

Charlie had gone to see Conal's rescued fox cub. As soon as he returned he got back to work. I could see him kneeling in the undergrowth at the edge of the orchard.

'Campanula,' he said, consulting Birtwhistle. 'Hey, top genes. Temperature *or* day length can make it flower. That could be important.'

Just then Eva came out of the orchard. A man walked beside her. He held himself away from the greenery around him, actually shuddering when a tangle of vines sprang back and brushed his face. His aura was compressed to a thin dark line. Why was he holding himself in like that? They didn't notice Charlie at first.

'It's a fair-sized plot,' said the man, 'it will take a lot of work to clear of course, neglected as it is, but I'm willing to make you a good offer.'

'What would you do with it, if you don't mind me asking?' Eva said.

'Some low building, paved terraces—tidy, nothing like the present eyesore.'

'Wildness has its charm.'

'In certain circumstances,' he said, and moved one of Eva's straying curls away from her eye. Eva looked surprised and the man straightened up. 'Control it or it will control you,' he said, 'Look at it—straining to break out.'

He smacked the vine down from in front of his face.

Then he leaned towards Eva again and spoke in a low voice: 'I know how hard it is for a woman on her own. If you need to talk, don't forget I'm in the next office.' He cleared his throat. 'Right, I'll send a formal offer in writing and we'll take it from there.'

Charlie shot up suddenly from the flowerbed. 'But Mum…' Eva shushed him as she guided the man away.

Charlie waited for her in the kitchen, his face set for battle.

'Why?' he said as soon as she returned.

'Sweetheart, we don't have a choice. You've noticed how tight things have been getting lately, haven't you? It was hard even before your dad left. Since the oil wars, the prices seem to double every week. If Mr Sperrin makes a good offer for the Jungle, it could solve all our money problems for years. Look at this,' Eva picked up his school sweatshirt, 'the elbows are gone, the collar's frayed. I'm ashamed to send you to school in it.'

'Mum, that's so not important. Everybody's the same.

The teachers understand. What about the Jungle? What about the animals and the birds and plants? It's their home.'

Eva looked at him questioningly. 'I know how much you love the garden, I love it too, but...'

'No, really, life is at stake. Do you want to sell it?'

'No.'

'Don't then, because I'd rather starve.'

'Charlie, it's not just the Jungle. If I don't pay something on the mortgage soon we could lose the whole house. It doesn't make sense anyway, the two of us living in a place this size.'

Charlie looked at me and I looked back. Our thoughts panicked and tumbled together. My roots braced as though against a coming gale.

'We can sell stuff, sell the car; it's no use without petrol. Then you can trade our petrol vouchers. I've heard people say they're worth more than money. You can sell all my stuff; my computer, all my games.'

'You'd do that to keep the garden?'

'I'd do anything.'

Eva didn't really believe that, but she couldn't see what I saw. The will in him was absolute; his aura split into defiant shells extending halfway across the room.

Both were silent for a minute.

'You must mind, not having all the things we used to have?' Eva said.

'No. It's fun growing our own food, and making stuff instead of buying it, and I like candles, and toast on the fire.'

'Yes, we still have fun don't we, but—you must miss something from the old days.'

He blinked hard.

'Come here, I'm sorry. Can you understand, joining that band—your dad is only following his dream?'

Charlie softened. He knew all about dreams.

'If only life was like monopoly,' she said, 'I could run round and round the board passing GO,' and she started running round the kitchen table, 'keep grabbing my money,' she snatched at imaginary cash, 'two hundred, I'll take that, thank you, round and round, not stopping till my annuities mature—if I had some, and I knew what they were.' She stopped, out of breath. Charlie was laughing now.

I recalled an exchange between myself and Wilfred. He had launched into one of his rants: 'Humans, they're such vain, puffed-up know-it-alls; yet they've only got five senses and those are pathetic: a hawk sees further, a dog's nose is so good he can tell where I walked last week, a bee can see in ultra-violet, birds and fish navigate half the planet without maps or compasses but none of them make a song and dance about it.'

I could see him working himself up into one of his fits. He goes rigid sometimes and lies there like he's dead; a dangerous thing for an animal. They have to stay guarded. I tried to distract him.

'I've noticed six,' I said.

'Six what?'

'Senses. Humans have another sense.'

'What would that be?' he said, scornful but interested.

'It's a sense that only humans have,' I said, stringing him along; it was rare enough for me to be telling him something.

His muscles started to relax. 'Well?'

'They have a sense of humour.'

He eyed me suspiciously. 'What's that?'

It's something you pick up if you study them for long enough. Ever heard them laugh, that ha-ha thing they do?

'Of course I have. I wasn't born yesterday. It's just part of their language.'

'No, it's more than that. They do it when certain kinds of things happen. I don't understand it yet but it's one of the things that makes them them, and us us.'

'And what use is it?'

'I don't know.'

'Does it help them survive?'

'Maybe,' I said, 'I'm still figuring it out.'

I knew one thing: no matter how terrible things were, someone would make a joke about it. I thought that was definitely worth a notch on the human side of the trunk.

Eva said she would put off selling for as long as possible, but I decided to keep an eye on her anyway. I didn't want any more surprises.

'Due, overdue, very overdue, pay up or go to court,' she said as she sorted the mail one morning. 'Right, bin those. What do I do about this?'

There was one envelope left to open. 'You don't look like a bill,' she said, 'or are you a bill in disguise?'

Eva opened the envelope and began to read. She frowned, shook her head in disbelief, sat back in the chair, staring, picked up the letter, and read it again.

'Well, damn you whoever you are,' she said holding the envelope to the light and looking at the postmark. She picked up the phone.

'Brigid, hi. Can you talk? Something creepy is going on,' I heard her say, then she walked out of the room so I missed the crucial bit. Some time later she came back still talking, 'Yeah, you're right, as if I haven't got enough worries. Anyway, I've got to get to work now, thanks for listening.'

She stood with her hands on her hips looking straight at me for quite a long time. I felt like she was looking to me for answers. 'Something will come up,' I said, because that's what Les Durrell said on *Brooke Farm* after the foot and mouth outbreak.

'Something will come up,' Eva said, then she glanced at her watch and ran out.

6

No Money No Cry

A red and green parrot flew overhead. It seemed to be laughing. Wilfred scampered into the garden.

'Freedom!' he saluted the parrot as it turned to a dot in the sky. 'I hope he makes it.'

'Where's he going?' I asked.

'Home to Senegal. The humans kidnapped him, wrenched him squawking from the nest, sent him thousands of miles stuffed in an airless box, and put him behind bars. For what crime? I just freed him. It's a long way home, but he's got directions and there'll be help on the way.'

'Why would people do something like that?'

'For money at one end, amusement at the other. They do love their amusement. It's usually pointless, wasteful or cruel of course. I've seen the idiots strapped to chunks of metal getting whirled around down at the old fairground. Now that's shut down they've gone back to tormenting the donkeys. Why? The business of life is enough for the rest of us.'

He gave me time to ponder all this.

'What if they wanted to help the parrot, to give it a better life?'

He looked at me in despair. 'Let me know when you run out of excuses,' he said, and he was off on another mission to bring down vermanity.

I kept brooding on what he'd said, and when Charlie came out later his words were scrambled into a noise I no longer understood.

'Pttii tmmm,' he seemed to say. 'Did you hear me? It's party time.'

He was carrying strawberries and ice-cream, candles, and a net of scraps for Morwen, the blackbird.

'Don't worry, Ash,' he said, 'I've got something for you too.'

I watched with interest as Charlie tipped the dark brown liquid around my roots.

'This is Brigid's secret formula. It's what she feeds to her prize veg,' he told me.

The slurry soaked quickly down and hit me with a rush.

'What's up, Ash—speechless? Well, is it good?'

'It beats the sap out of manure.'

'I'll tell Brigid; she will be pleased,' he said through his laughter.

As I wallowed, Charlie climbed up and toasted the garden. He had sorted all his papers into a smart green file, as thick as Birtwhistle. He held it up proudly.

'I declare phase one of the project—the Jungle register, to be complete. This garden is all present, correct, and ready for the call.'

'What's phase two?' I asked.

'I don't know for certain. It's cooking up somewhere. Like clouds brew out of sight.'

I was too happy to question any further. I had Charlie to myself again and Brigid's feed was making me feel like Les Durrell after six pints at the Tipsy Tup. Wilfred's words faded away.

My good mood lasted well into the next day. Charlie was due home from school so I watched the kitchen and waited.

Eva was walking up and down, opening and shutting empty cupboard doors. She fished in the bread crock, pulled out a bag containing three slices and threw it on the table. Scribbling down some figures she counted under her breath then stared at the figures again. I heard Charlie coming in. Eva straightened up, brushed some wetness from her cheekbone with the heel of her hand, and turned with a smile.

'Did you have a good time?'

'Brilliant,' he grabbed Eva's sleeve, 'and guess what? Come and look, Conal's got a horse and cart. We're all going for a ride.'

'Whose clothes are you wearing?'

'Conal's—I got changed to clear out the pigs. Come on, they're waiting for us.'

I wondered if Charlie knew how much I looked forward to him coming home.

The door slammed. My trunk felt hollow with disappointment. I heard clopping, slow at first, then picking up speed and fading. The clops came back as they passed down Spring Hill. I saw the cart where the hedge dipped, and glimpsed Charlie's ruffled hair. My mind strained after them and I felt a familiar pang, knowing that as long as I lived I could never leave the garden.

Miffed, I turned to Holly. 'I wonder what it's really like to be an animal,' I said. 'There's one thing I envy them. I'd like to ease my roots out, shake the soil off and go for a stroll.'

'Horrible thought,' said Holly, 'I feel dizzy just thinking about it.'

'It's disturbing, but get past that falling feeling and imagine the freedom. You know where I'd go on my stroll, I'd go and have a proper look at the sea.'

From the garden the sea is a strip of blue that hazes into sky. Gulls land on the roof sometimes and I smell the sea on them. Once a gull got dusted with my pollen and my thoughts launched from the roof with it. I was riding and sliding, tipping and balancing on air, heading for the wide open sea. Then I lost the connection. I've since found out more about the sea from TV.

'I'll tell you what blows me away,' I went on, 'there's a whole other world under there. Did you know that the sea has its own birds, called fish; and its own special gardens where all the plants are weeds—seaweeds? I like that, it's a great leveller.'

The clock in the sitting room changed to 7:00. Those

symbols meant it was time for *Brooke Farm*, and still they hadn't returned. At the end of the last episode, Sally Durrell's sister had stolen her sleeping pills. It was a coma waiting to happen. Did they have to choose that day to miss the programme?

The garden waited but the screen stayed dark and dumb. It was over to Rose, my best imagination student, to make up the story for us. Rose is a bit of a one-trick peony; her solution is always to kill people off, whereas in real life I've found that they just go into comas. This happens all the time in the soaps. It's like seeds lying dormant. Dormant seeds can be woken by a change in the weather. Dormant people, however, can only be woken by visits from footballers.

As Rose finished her story, the door slammed. They were back. Eva had a fresh flush and Charlie's eyes shone even more brightly than usual.

'That was great; can we have a horse?'

Eva rolled her eyes.

'Well, chickens then. Brigid said she's going to let us have some hens.'

'She gives us too much; I must do something to pay her back. Have you eaten?'

Charlie's too sensitive not to notice the over-brightness in her voice. He looked at the thin bread bag on the table.

'Yes,' he said, 'loads.'

I saw her relax. Come on then, we'll have an hour of telly before bed.

There were six minutes of *Brooke Farm* left. I was

right. It was a classic coma storyline: the tubes, the steadily beeping screen by the bed, a sinister shadow falling across the pillow and then the theme tune. Only then did I notice Eva's lack of interest. Her eyes were focused somewhere else and under the music I could hear the low rumbling of Charlie's empty stomach. They continued to sit through a game show, lost in their own thoughts. At last Eva got up heavily. As she followed Charlie upstairs he asked a question:

'Mum, Conal's dad saw you in town this afternoon. Did you have a day off?'

Eva sighed. 'I might as well tell you, my hours have been cut. I don't get it; I'm the best worker in the office. Why not chatty Cathy or idle Ivor?'

They sat down on Charlie's bed.

'Anyway, I don't want you worrying,' she said, pushing his hair back and looking into his eyes. 'We can still sell the Jungle if we have to.'

Charlie closed his eyes.

'Listen to me a minute. Mr Sperrin stopped by my desk today to remind me.'

'No-oo,' said Charlie, putting his hands over his ears and rolling on the bed in a mock fit. 'He can't have the Jungle; he'll ruin it. It won't be jungly any more.'

Children speak in childish words but the pictures in their heads may not be childish at all. In Charlie's head I saw something terrible: a crumpling down of all that was green into a grey, rotting wasteland; birds and insects trapped in the slime and then, nothing.

'Listen. I said no, but...'

'But what?'

'He made me a better offer—silly money, probably double what it's worth.'

'What did you say then?' Charlie asked intently.

'I said I needed time to think.'

'Oh,' he let out an agonised little sob. 'If you sell, I'll camp in it. I'll live in the trees.'

'Why does it mean so much to you?'

'Mum, it's everything.'

Eva looked bemused.

'Listen, the garden is alive.'

'I know that.'

'No you don't. It's alive like we are, and it has to go on. It's the mother and father of everything that comes after...after the changes.'

Again Charlie's thoughts flew high above Eva's.

'Eva, are you there?' It was Brigid's voice.

'Come up.'

'I've brought your uniform, Charlie. You left it at ours.' Brigid hovered in the doorway.

Charlie spied an ally. 'Mum's hours have been cut and now she wants to sell the Jungle.'

'Not wants, needs.'

'I knew something was wrong. What's it all about then?' Brigid said, sitting on the bed.

Eva explained. 'Sperrin's obsessed with our trees. He was always asking Pete to cut them back. He said they blocked his light and the roots were making his house sink. But you know what Pete's like: 'What's eating you, man? Chill out,' he used to say. Anyway, Sperrin can't wait to get rid of the trees now, though he says he just wants to help me out.'

'I'd hold on to it if you can,' Brigid said, 'land will be the only thing worth having soon. Money's no use when there's nothing left to buy, but you can live off your land.'

Charlie bounced up on his knees, the speckles dancing in his eyes: 'Yeah, who needs money anyway? Let's do without it.'

'You have some good ideas, but that's not one of them,' Eva said.

'All right then, let's see how long we can live without money. If we can last for thirty days then we don't sell. Is it a deal?' He was on his feet now bouncing manically, his hair lifting and flopping.

'Good lad,' said Brigid, 'I'm behind you all the way.'

'Look Charlie,' Eva said, taking him by the shoulders, 'I can't promise anything, but…all right, let's give it a go.'

'Starting tomorrow,' Charlie said. He was good at hope.

7

Swap Shop

I was all for it. Every living thing except humans manages without money. It seemed to me that money was nothing but trouble, a bad habit they needed to break.

Eva couldn't see it. When her shoe flapped away from the upper, she thought in the old way.

'I'm going to have to buy shoes,' she told Charlie apologetically.

'Wait there,' he said. A few minutes later he came back with a box. 'Twenty-three pairs—from the attic.'

'I can't wear those,' she said.

'It's these or your wellies. Look, do this and I'll…I'll tidy my room.'

Eva turned slowly. 'How long since I first asked you to tidy your room?'

''Bout three years.'

'Okay, what do you think for work: blue platforms or yellow stilettos?'

'I like the cowboy boots,' said Charlie.

'Here's to the death of fashion,' she said resignedly.

Next day Eva wavered again. 'It's the final demand from the electricity company, and I've got seven days to pay something on the mortgage.'

I could see that in her heart she'd given up. She was just playing along with Charlie, waiting for him to get real.

'All right,' said Charlie, 'stay cool. I'll think of something.'

Charlie thought. He thought in circles as he walked round and round the garden. 'We're not selling,' he said to the Jungle, as he paced the edge of the orchard. 'Staying,' he chanted as he swung backwards and forwards on the treehouse rope, till I told him the friction was burning my bark.

That night was barely cooler than the day had been. Eva came out late to inhale.

'Beauteous,' she whispered. Charlie knelt by his bedroom window.

'Mum,' he called, 'Can I come down? I can't sleep.'

'Come. Ten minutes.'

They sat on the back step together.

'Why can't you sleep?' She put an arm round him and he leaned against her shoulder.

'Kids don't have a say in anything, do they? They're just meant to put up with things.'

'Well, if the grown-ups do the thinking, you can get on and have fun.'

'It doesn't work like that though, does it?'

'Maybe not.'

They murmured together until the sudden dimming of curfew. The stars grinned as night in its fullness came down, and Eva said they should go to bed.

Charlie reappeared in his room and I watched him, a spinning hump under a quilt. Too hot, he threw the quilt back, too cold he pulled a corner of it back. At last he came and leaned his elbows on the window again.

'Want to play the breathing game?' I suggested.

'I'll try,' he said with a sigh.

This is a relaxing game we play which often ends with Charlie drifting off to sleep and me slipping off into my own tree rest. I breathe out and Charlie takes in my green breath; he breathes out and I take in his red breath. The molecules bubbling in my leaves get sucked in a stream towards Charlie. He says it's like a pure green drink; it makes him feel like he's growing. Charlie's lungs have branches just like a tree; a mysterious pink-lit tree, and to me his breath tastes of life in a warm, mineral way. Try it some time: pick a friendly tree and breathe with it; it's very relaxing, aah...

'That's it,' he murmured after a while, 'that's what I'll do. Thanks, Ash,' and he slept.

Charlie was up and out at dawn, whispering to the garden that he needed their help. He would do everything in his power to save the Jungle, but, for thirty days at least, the garden must provide.

The garden came through. Every day after school Charlie set up a stall in front of the house selling veg and flowers from the garden. We all rallied round and the more he picked the more we blossomed. Charlie filled a bowl with pea pods, and new pods appeared faster than they could be eaten. Stems bowed to the ground with fruits; roots and tubers swelled with goodness. Word got around the neighbourhood. The flowers were bigger and more colourful than anyone had ever seen. The veg was sweet and crisp and curiously vitalizing.

When Wilfred next came to the garden he could barely push his way through the veg plot.

'What's going on with this garden?' he asked as he stripped a pod of peas. 'I've never seen greens taking off like this, and, um, so sweet. What's that gardener of yours feeding you?'

'Same as always,' I said.

'I don't think so. Just look at it.'

As I looked around the other gardens and then back to ours, it was clear. We burgeoned. We were greener, brighter, bigger, stronger. In the patchwork of countryside and gardens, we glowed with a powerful green and golden halo.

'That's Charlie's doing, I guess,' I told him.

'Oh yes. Clever boy, that.'

'Yes, he's got plans for the garden.'

Wilfred was very still, listening intently; too intently.

'I don't really know what they are yet,' I said truthfully.

'Well, when you do, I'll be interested,' Wilfred said, 'there's something unusual happening here.'

On Saturday morning Charlie hauled down some boxes from the attic to add to his stall. I couldn't see but Charlie was close enough for me to tune in to him. He wrestled with Eva who clutched a bundle to her chest.

'We don't need them,' he said.

'But they're your baby clothes.'

'Yes, all of them. Just keep one thing if you have to.'

She picked through them sulkily. 'You're heartless.'

Conal came to help. 'You let that mirror go for how much?' he said with his Irish lilt. 'Move over now, let me show you how it's done.'

I'm fond of Conal. His instinct for animals is like Charlie's feeling for plants. If an animal is sick, he knows exactly what to do. Brigid always sends him to fetch the animal feeds because, she says, he haggles like some wily old farmer.

Conal cleared the table and Charlie filled it up again. They brought the spoils into the kitchen. This money, Charlie reasoned, was okay to spend because it didn't come out of Eva's wages.

Later he was peering at the electricity meter and copying down the numbers.

'We're going to halve this,' he said, and he handed Eva a list of rules.

She read: 'Ironing, don't bother. Hoovering, once a month will do. Kettle, get used to cold drinks. Standby, banned. Washing, just rub dirt off dirty bits. Is that us or the clothes?'

'Both.'

At least she managed a smile. Later on she got jumpy. Every time her hand drifted towards a switch, Charlie appeared beside her with his clipboard. 'On a scale of 1-10, how necessary is that?' he asked.

'Ten being?'

'Life or death.'

'How high does it have to be before you let me use it?'

'Ten. Come on, we can do it; we're used to power cuts.'

He was a bit more lax when it came to telly, but I had to protest when he switched off *Brooke Farm* halfway through.

'Don't stress,' he said, 'it's just the commercials. We're down to an hour of telly, and if we switch off between programmes we can save twelve minutes of electricity per day, which is seventy-three hours per year, which, if everybody did it, would be about 219 million hours of electricity saved per year.'

He did test my patience with that one.

'Now,' I kept butting in, 'switch on now.'

'Not yet, not yet,' he laughed, '3,2,1—now,' and mostly he got it right.

The mortgage company gave Eva four more weeks to pay. Charlie smiled as he marked another money-free day on the calendar.

'Eleven down, nineteen to go,' he said.

'Hmm, what shall we buy first on day thirty?' Eva asked.

'Sweets,' Charlie forgot himself; sweets are his weakness, 'but I can wait—easily.'

'I could kill for some chocolate myself. Do you fancy a walk to the shop? We can spare a few pence, I'm sure.'

'You're a weak-willed woman. www. Mum. I know,' he said suddenly. Jumping up, he dragged a kitchen stool in front of the cupboards and reached for an old biscuit tin.

'Ah-ha,' he said as he prised it open.

Inside were some bits of smashed Easter egg, half a stick of rock in a twist of cellophane, turquoise jelly beans, and some Christmas cake icing with the marzipan stuck inside.

'But that's all the stuff we don't like. It's been there for ages.'

'Remember that experiment we did, when Dad said all jelly beans tasted the same if you closed your eyes; well he was right. Close your eyes: this isn't a turquoise jelly bean, this is an electric blue paradise island sweet.'

'Mmm,' she said, 'and this is scrumptious sticky chewy nougat,' and she fed Charlie a chunk of seaside rock, gone soft on the outside. And this is my favourite chocolate truffle.' She ate a broken piece of Easter egg.

'Yes, and I bet we could grind up this icing and make some cookies.'

'Cookies,' Eva growled.

They carried on, eating their way through most of the tin, giving all the sweets exotic names; then they came out into the garden on a sugar rush.

Clouds were just parting on blue. The leaves were all cupping rain water after a heavy shower.

'Fresh,' Eva said ecstatically as she inhaled. She was standing under a sapling at the edge of the orchard with her eyes closed. Charlie sneaked behind her and shook the tree. Eva's curly hair was flattened and her shoulders were darkened with rain water.

'You,' she said scarily, and chased Charlie round the garden until he let her catch him.

'Look, look,' he said, 'you can do it to me,' and she did, and they laughed. But I saw what they didn't see, which was Graham standing on his side of the hedge, like me, just watching.

8

The Street Meet

In spite of all our efforts, on day sixteen a man came to turn off the electricity supply.

'Well that's it,' Eva said, 'we did our best, but we can't carry on.'

'Just give me another day,' Charlie begged.

He came up to the treehouse and waited for inspiration. 'Like leaves on a tree,' he said at length, 'we're all like leaves on a tree.'

His next idea was helped along by the government. Humans have things called governments. I think they are like sheepdogs which nose everybody onto certain paths, though they can also be like nasty guard dogs. The government had started putting up posters and sending out leaflets with slogans like, 'Don't do it alone', and 'Energy—it's for sharing', and there were pictures of group bake-ins, TV parties, and car sharing. Everyone in the pictures was smiling.

Charlie made his own leaflet and showed it to Eva.

'Street Meet. Swap, Share and Save,' she read. She looked questioningly at Charlie.

'So you want to invite all the neighbours round here for a meeting, on Friday.'

'Yes, so we can help each other survive.' Eva raised her eyebrows. 'That's how it will be.'

Up till then I had seen about twenty humans up close. All at once there was another twenty.

The thing with humans is that, though they seem pretty much identical, if you look carefully you notice subtle differences. Trees are obviously different, with different numbers of branches in different arrangements, and trunks and roots which twist and fork in endless ways. You could never mistake one tree for another. Humans all have two arms, two legs, a head. It takes practice to tell them apart—then you notice little things like the cleft in Eva's chin, and how Conal's freckles run together. Eyes, though, are the giveaway; eyes are never alike.

Seeing all those new faces I'm afraid I got over-excited.

'Look at that one,' I said to Holly, 'I've never seen anything like that before.'

'Like what?' said Holly.

'No hair at all—head like a potato.'

'Hmm,' said Holly, and she went back to contemplating the clouds.

'Oh look, there's a brand new one. Look, look, look!'

'Is that a human shoot?' said Holly.

'It's called a baby,' I said.

Eva actually frowned up at the window then, because I, in my eagerness, was blocking out the light.

Soon every chair and cushion was taken. Everyone joked about how bad things were. I watched closely as strangers knit into neighbours.

By the time that the meeting was over Charlie had made a list of skills and surplus stuff that people were willing to swap. He also made a deal with Graham next door.

A long wire appeared. It came out of Graham's window, tightened across my trunk, passed through our kitchen window and ran up to the washing machine. Eva flicked it on and sighed with relief as it started to churn. In return Eva handed a big box of fruit and veg over the hedge to Graham.

Eva seemed to try harder after that. She could see that everyone was struggling and that they would have to help each other. Charlie was right; from then on, that's how it would be. And she had another reason for keeping going.

Animals have this padding on their branches: they call it fat, it's protection and a food store. Eva was losing hers and for some reason this seemed to please her. 'You should be worried,' I said, 'never know when you're going to need those fat stores,' but she just stood in front of the long mirror and held her loose jeans away from her flat stomach with a satisfied smile.

Charlie put a big red cross through day thirty and high-fived Eva.

He came to the window and looked at the garden.

'See, I said I wouldn't desert you,' I heard him think. He turned back to Eva.

'Now, do you promise not to sell the Jungle?'

'I can't promise. But *if* things stay as they are *and* we get the power back on soon, then I think we'll manage. Is that okay?'

He nodded.

During the experiment they had learned to live almost like trees I thought with satisfaction; they ate and drank and breathed and seemed content. Except for one thing.

Every morning they sat at the breakfast table listening. If the postman passed the door Eva looked relieved. If the letter box rattled, a light came into Charlie's eyes but Eva's face tightened. It wasn't just bills she dreaded. I suspected it also had to do with that letter hidden under the bread bin. But it all came out soon enough.

9

Signs of Rot

It was Violet's turn to host the street meet. Violet's house is three down from ours. I can't see in directly but one of my seedlings is growing in her garden, allowing me to catch snatches of the meet in a foggy, distant way. There was Violet, a bent figure in a headscarf, and checked slippers with bobbles on. She looked flushed and excited: all those people in her lonely, slow-ticking house.

I was getting to know the characters in the street and looked forward to the meets in our house. If Wilfred would just watch and listen as I did, he must see that people were mostly good.

The meet went through the usual business. The car keepers were named for the month, and the cooking and washing partners.

'Right,' said Bob, 'well that wraps it up for tonight. I'd like to thank Vi for a nice cup of tea. Is there any other business?'

Eva stood up. 'Yes there is.' There was an expectant hush: 'It seems as though I've offended someone around here. I've been getting letters—nasty letters.' She unfolded some papers with a shaking hand. 'Listen to this:

' "Witch, you are a disgrace to the neighbourhood. Your garden festers with foul smells, disease and rats. Your brat boy has been seen trespassing. All your neighbours want you out. Do yourself a favour and leave." ' She unfolded another piece of paper: ' "Still here witch, what are you waiting for, someone to push you? It can be arranged." '

Who would write that? All the neighbours seemed so nice. But Wilfred said that all humans have rot in their hearts. A doubt flickered in me.

Eva went on, 'There's more. The thing is, there are things in these letters which only a neighbour could know—a close neighbour, someone who…watches me; so, whoever it is, stand up now; tell me face to face what it is you've got against me.'

'This is not right,' said a muffled voice inside my trunk.

It was Charlie. I had trained myself to tune in to Charlie's thoughts over ever greater distances. If I focused really hard I could even reach him in school, but only in snatches. Now I was picking him up in the Jungle, right down on the Sperrin's border.

I could see the summer Jungle brimming with life. The tall wire fence erected by Sperrin barely held it in. Trees and bushes pushed up against it, making it bulge in places. On the other side was strict, clipped order. Sperrin's hobby was topiary. All around his house was a high hedge clipped like a castle wall, inside this were two more banks of castellated hedge and three gateways guarded by privet dogs, soldiers, stags, bears and other works in progress. Sperrin snipped at his bushes obsessively; not a stray leaf was allowed to follow its nature and reach for the sun. The ever-present snip-snip grated under my bark.

Charlie was examining the ancient stone wall which ran on our side of Sperrin's fence. It was a micro-garden all by itself; shallow roots somehow found crumbs on which to flourish; it had its own springy lawns of moss and mottles of acid yellow lichen. A fine thing, the old wall. *Junglus slaterii* sprouted from a gap in the stones. Charlie stroked its furry, purple-tipped leaves.

'Come on,' Conal called, 'I'm sending the sweets over?'

Conal sat astride Sycamore and Charlie climbed to a fork in Chestnut. They had rigged up an aerial system with a bucket attached so that they could send things from tree to tree. Charlie was sending sherbet strawberries over to Conal when the rope came loose and sent the bucket flying over into Sperrin's garden where it clanged and bumped across his lawn.

'Oh, nice one,' said Conal, looking down at the rusty old bucket.

Sperrin looked up from his clipping and walked over. He was tight-lipped but smiled as he came near. He held the bucket on one finger.

'Now boys, I suppose you want this back. I'm going to have to ask you to be more considerate. Mrs Sperrin is a nervous type and boys give her headaches.'

He handed the bucket up to Charlie. 'Better get down from there, we don't want any accidents, do we?' and he laughed a forced, hollow laugh.

The human laugh is an odd thing, but it's a sound that normally lifts my spirits. Sperrin's laugh was barren.

'That's right; off you go. Plenty of room to play without coming down here,' he called as the boys backed away.

Something was bothering Charlie. He paused and looked back as if he needed to check something but there was nothing to see. Sperrin had gone.

'It's empty,' said Conal taking the bucket, 'and my mouth's watering for that sherbet. I cleaned the chickens for a month to get those. It'll be another month before we get any more. Will we go back and look for them?'

They turned. There was a scattering of pink and a glint of cellophane in the grass just beyond the fence.

'We can reach those,' said Conal, 'all we need is a stick with a bit of a hook in it.'

Conal found the stick quickly and lay on his belly in a narrow gap where the old wall had broken down in front of the wire fence. The stick was too short.

'If I make a little hollow I'll get my arm under here; that's it.'

The stick advanced towards the sweets and hooked around them.

Quick as a snake, a hand shot out and clamped over Conal's wrist.

'Trespass!' Sperrin shouted from where he lay behind the wall, 'It's trespass.' He came up onto his knees, still clamping Conal's forearm to the ground, and breathing heavily.

'Now listen carefully. All of this is mine,' he gestured from the fence and beyond; 'all of this,' he indicated the length of Conal's arm, 'shouldn't be here. If this was a branch the law says I could cut it off'—that peculiar laugh again.

There was something very odd about Sperrin's mouth. He had inside-out lips like a fish. His eyes too were fishy: cold and bulbous. At that moment they were excited and undisguised.

'So that's who you are,' thought Charlie.

Conal stood up, showing a hump on his back. The bump rippled along his shoulders, round his middle, down one leg and up the other.

'Good god, what's that?' said Sperrin.

A white head with pink eyes erupted from the top of Conal's jumper. Sperrin spluttered and staggered backwards.

Conal giggled, 'It's only Elsie. She's a ferret. Why don't you stroke her?'

'A stinking polecat—it's disgusting.'

'No, she's beautiful,' Charlie said.

'Insolent. I'll be speaking to your mother, though it's a father's hand you need—a proper father.'

Charlie froze. I felt it. His heart and brain just froze,

and so I lost him.

The room took a breath and murmured. Eva's eyes went deliberately round, pausing for a moment on each face. Some looked sympathetic; some looked offended; some, trying too hard to look innocent, ended up looking guilty.

'Come on, whoever did this, have the guts to stand up for yourself.'

There were mutters of sympathy round the room. Bob put his arm round Eva and water came out of her eyes.

The room grew very dark to me. I saw shapes crowding round Eva, then Charlie and Conal came in and pushed their way forward. I lost the picture but faintly caught a little voice saying: 'What's wrong with Mum?'

When they got home Charlie asked why Eva hadn't told him about the letters.

'I didn't want to worry you.'

Charlie came to the window and looked past me to the Jungle. After a while he spoke.

'Mum, did you know that Mr Sperrin hates kids?'

'What are you talking about?'

'It's true.'

'Don't be silly. He's got none of his own—probably doesn't understand them.' Charlie raised his eyebrows.

'You think he wrote the letters don't you?' she said. 'No, it doesn't fit, he's being so helpful at work.'

Next morning there was another envelope. Like the others it was pale blue with a typed address.

Eva's hand shook as she held it. 'I've a good mind to put it straight on the fire,' she said.

'Let's see what it says,' said Charlie, 'it might give us some clues.'

Tight-mouthed, Eva slit it open and swore. 'Now I'm really confused.'

A bundle of money spilled out of the envelope. A typed strip came with it. It said simply 'wishing you well'. Charlie looked at the note so closely he went cross-eyed, then he sniffed. 'Nice smell—like fresh washing,' he said.

'What am I supposed to do with this?' She held up the fan of notes. 'Do you think...would it be all right to pay the electricity bill?'

'Well, it doesn't *feel* like bad money,' Charlie said thoughtfully.

10

I Spy

I had my first rebellious thought whilst watching *Brooke Farm*. Father Parry, a wise man in a long black dress and a white collar, had said to a crowd of well-dressed people, all very full of themselves: 'Are any of you dressed as well as a lily?'

'Obviously not,' I had muttered from my viewing point outside the lounge window, 'so how about a bit of respect?'

Charlie had swung one eye towards me and started with a fit of giggles.

'Good,' said Wilfred, when I told him about this, 'you're beginning to see through them—there's hope for you yet.'

And he followed up quickly by telling me the nastiest things he could think of. I don't even want to repeat them. 'So you see,' he said, 'there are humans who like causing pain: to other humans, to animals, even to themselves. They like it. I'll leave you with that thought.'

I didn't believe it. Until I remembered that friend of Charlie's, George, stabbing the earwig. Then I happened to look through next door's window.

I watched in horror as Graham attacked the other man with a drill, and in the most cowardly way possible, surprising him from behind.

Charlie came thudding down the chute.

'What's up, Ash?' he said. 'You don't seem like yourself.'

I quickly shut him out of my thoughts. A child shouldn't see what I had just seen.

'I'm okay.'

'Half the school field got ploughed up today. The school's going to grow all its own veg and all the kids get to help—that's good, isn't it?'

'Mmm,' I said absently. The vermin score raced forwards in my mind.

'Charlie, if you feel like something bad is about to happen and you keep on thinking about it, is that worry?'

'I'd say so.'

'Then I'm worried.'

'What are you worried about, Ash?'

'It feels like we've got enemies on every side.'

'I feel it too.'

'Sperrin, I saw his aura; it's black—I've never seen anything like it before.'

'And Mum still trusts him.'

'Then there's Graham.'

'What about him?'

‘I think there might be a hidden side to him.’

Charlie sighed. ‘There’s only one thing Graham’s hiding.’ He fiddled with some plant fibre string he’d been making. ‘There’s Mum,’ he said and slid down the rope without saying goodbye.

I turned to Holly. ‘Did I say something wrong?’

‘Give up,’ she said, ‘you’ll never understand them,’ and she dropped back into a sun trance.

I looked into Graham’s house again, dreading what I might see, but the room was empty. It was Eva’s strange behaviour that drew me back to the kitchen.

‘Nnaaargh,’ she shouted, as she threw her bag down. Then she punched a pile of washing and stamped like a toddler throwing a tantrum.

11

Here Comes the Chopper

Charlie and Eva were helping Graham with his garden.

'I don't know where I'm going wrong,' Graham said. 'You must have a magic touch,' and his eyes wandered to our lush greenery.

Eva bent to Graham's grey, hard-packed soil. 'All this needs to be broken up. The plants can't push their roots through it and they need water.' She stood up straight, throwing back the weight of her curls.

I was just learning to read human body language. Children mostly tell it like it is, adults hardly ever. The truth is in their eyes and faces and gestures and movements; you just have to learn the codes. Graham was smiling too much and breathing high up in his chest. What did that mean? Charlie seemed to know. He moved between them.

'You said you had something to show me,' he said to Graham.

'Yeah. My pride and joy. Wait there.'

'Well, I'll get off then,' Eva said, handing Graham a calendar of things he needed to do.

'Go, go, go,' I shouted to Charlie.

'Stop being so para,' Charlie hissed at me, 'check his aura; he's okay.'

'Clever enough to hide the rot?' I said.

Graham came out wheeling a gleaming metallic monster of a bike. Cherished it was; every bit of it polished to perfection; not a fingerprint dulled its long stretches of silver; not a scratch marred its buffed leather.

'Sickening,' I said, 'all that attention lavished on a dead thing, while your poor plants are on their last legs.'

'This is what I bought when I sold my slopes to the Sperrins,' Graham boasted. 'It's a Harley V-pod. I've had it for two years and it still makes me shiver. Look at those lines. I was going to take it round the world. Then the war broke out. It looks like I'll never get to do it now.'

'I haven't seen you ride it.'

'No, I will, but it's got to be for a big enough reason. I wouldn't go burning petrol for pleasure. And I wouldn't use it for a trip to the shops; that would belittle the spirit of the beast. For now, I just polish it and dream my petrol-head dreams.'

Graham lowered himself reverently onto the seat, and cocked his head towards the pillion.

'Climb on. Can you feel the power, hear that exhaust growl, see the road stretching away through the rocks, surf crashing?'

Graham swayed from side to side as though he was

taking bends, then bent low to the handlebars, like an awful demon.

Charlie slid to the ground. 'Well I hope you get to ride it again some day.'

'I don't kid myself. That whole way of life has gone now, hasn't it?'

'Yes,' said Charlie, kindly, as though he were talking to a child.

'Promise me you'll never go round there again by yourself,' I said when Charlie returned.

'Not unless you tell me why.'

'Just trust me.'

Eva came out and handed a bowl up to Charlie.

'Will you pick some berries while you're up there. I've found this old recipe for Rowan jelly.'

'Told you—whatever you need is in the garden,' Charlie said.

'Just as well,' Eva said darkly.

'Do you mind, Ash?' Charlie asked.

'Delighted; be my guest.'

'That's right: take, take, take. Don't leave any for the wild things,' said a voice from the hedge.

It was Wilfred. His behaviour had been strained and agitated for some weeks.

He had finally lost all patience with the human race he told me; it was time for action.

Charlie took the berries down to the kitchen and came back with Conal who carried a hen under each arm. Charlie was thrilled with Hilda and Gilda. He sat on the grass with Conal and threw corn to the birds.

Wilfred gnawed tetchily on a twig as he watched them.

'I wonder why they lay eggs,' Charlie said, 'I mean, when there's no baby chicken inside. It's just a waste of energy. It's like they've got a conveyor belt inside them, and it just keeps churning out eggs for no reason.'

'They do it for us, don't they?' Conal said, jokingly.

I saw Wilfred freeze; I saw him make himself large. I saw him start a slow advance towards Conal. I saw him bare his teeth.

'Wilfred, stop it! What are you thinking about?' I shouted.

He stopped in the undergrowth and looked up at me.

'Someone needs to tell them, while they're young, that animals do not exist just for their convenience,' he hissed.

'And how do you mean to do that? By biting him?'

'It's one way.'

'Not a way he'd understand.'

Charlie had noticed something. He was looking over to the undergrowth.

Wilfred shrank down and relaxed. A twinkle came into his eye.

'You're right,' he said, 'there are much better ways of making them listen. In fact it should be starting about now.'

'What are you up to?' I asked uneasily.

'Just commit to the cause and I'll tell all.'

And he slipped away leaving me stuck in the mud as usual.

Something wasn't right. Since the traffic had gone away, air was the new wine. It surprised people that breathing could be a pleasure. I felt the same. Everything had become faintly and subtly garden-scented. That evening the air was dirty again.

Charlie crouched on the floor rearranging the seed collection. I saw his back stiffen. He turned, came to the window and shuddered. I felt it too: it was a tremor which passed up from the whole garden. A tree shivering and rustling on a perfectly still night is an unnatural thing, but there it is, even Holly was shaking. Charlie grabbed his telescope, climbed as high into my branches as he could safely go, and looked across to the Jungle. In the round frame of the telescope this is what we saw.

There was Sperrin: on a warm night, all togged up in a boiler suit and mask, spraying poison from a gun. He'd fixed himself up with three different canisters attached to his suit, so that he could plug into the right poison for the job. Apparently he was after anything that crawls or flies, he was after weeds and he was after any plant that dared to cross the border between his garden and ours. Empty canisters were thrown aside as he strapped on new ones. After a few minutes every plant around was choking and wheezing as the poisons drifted over us.

But there was worse to come: creaking and cracking; my friends, Birch, Sycamore and Spruce, groaning;

branches whirling over the fence; Sperrin in a frenzy. I saw flashes of his purple face between the dark green pine fronds. He was twisting and thrashing about with the branches; not breaking them with a quick clean cut, but twisting them off, torturing Spruce and leaving ugly jagged ends. I couldn't watch; instead I took a look at Charlie's face. He was watching with big, still eyes that narrowed every time Spruce groaned. After he'd done with Spruce, Sperrin turned his frenzy against Sycamore and then Yew. When the sounds of splitting and cracking had finally stopped I took another look down the garden. Sperrin had pulled off his mask. Sweat poured down his face as he threw the last of the broken branches back into the Jungle. Then he did a victory spray of poison up into the air and strode back to his house.

Charlie slid down his rope and ran to the bottom of the Jungle. There, he went along, talking to the trees, climbing up where he could and inspecting the splintered stumps of branches.

Eva came out of the house to inhale just as Charlie burst out of the Jungle with twigs in his hair and that faint green tinge to his skin that I've noticed sometimes when he's been thinking like a tree thinks. He told Eva what had happened.

'Why did Mr Sperrin do that? Is it because I annoyed him the other day?'

'No,' said Eva, her eyes flashing angrily 'it's not you, it's me. I found this in the recycling bin yesterday.' She opened out some crumpled paper. 'It's a memo from

Sperrin to my boss: I have some confidential information re: E. Slater. Cannot disclose details but I advise that she is considered for the next round of job cuts. I went straight down to Sperrin's office like I'd got a rocket up my behind. I burst in, slammed the memo on his desk. "You liar," I said.

' "I was acting on instructions from higher up," he said. "Actually I've been trying to protect you. Trust me, and you'll never have to worry about money again." '

'I almost believed him, then I looked into his eyes.'

'You saw what I saw,' Charlie said.

'Yes, I knocked his hand off my shoulder. "You're a liar and a creep," I said. "Well guess what, you can kiss goodbye to any hopes you had of getting your hands on me or my land." '

'Yes!' said Charlie, punching the air.

'Job or no job,' Eva said quietly.

They sat down together against my trunk. I hung closely over them.

'We must be able to stop him doing things like that? Isn't it criminal damage or something?' Charlie asked.

'He has a right to cut off overhanging branches,' Eva said.

'But his face was like a madman's. Why is he so angry? It's only a few branches.'

'It's frustration I suppose; he knows he'll never get me to sell now.'

'It's like he feels threatened by the Jungle,' Charlie said.

'That's it,' I said, 'that's the top and bottom of it.

That's the inside and outside of it. Unfettered life scares him. He wants to control everything.'

Charlie's hand stole around and patted me.

I had seen it in Sperrin's face, a hatred of life: for him there was something terrible about the Jungle with its wild drifting seeds, its blowing leaves, its overhanging branches, invasive roots, scurryings, buzzings and flappings. That's why he hated children too I thought; it was the uncontrolled life in them.

They sat, quietly thoughtful. After a while Charlie asked, 'Will they sack you now?'

'They will if he has a say in it, unless I can get something on him. Information's what I need, because information is power,' and for a moment her eyes clouded and she looked quite scary. I was beginning to think that even the nicest of humans have a dark side to them. 'Come on, let's treat ourselves to some telly before lights out,' she said.

It wasn't the best night on TV. They watched a music programme called *Vintage Top of the Pops* because it showed Pete's moment of fame. Half his face appeared under a curtain of hair for a few seconds as he played guitar on one of the tracks. The programme changed to *Top of the Chops* in my mind because I was still thinking about my wounded friends. I drifted away to talk to them and only came back for the news, which was the same old story of who bombed what, and an interview with an ancient man. 'It's worse than the last war,' he quavered, 'people like me with no savings will be eating cats and dogs soon.'

I pictured the Sperrin's moggy, Adolf, being basted slowly on a spit, and heard Violet putting her cat, Maisie out. 'Go on, go on; out you go.' Light ran down the garden as she opened the door; there was a yowl as she chucked her out. Looked like she was feeling nervous too.

I listened to the best bit of the news, the 'now cheer up' spot.

'And finally,' said the news reader, 'reports are coming in from around the country of bizarre behaviour in the animal kingdom. At a Kent zoo, a keeper was held hostage by an orang utan, while dozens of other primates made their way to freedom. This report from nearby Rotham Woods:

' "I was out walking, when my dogs surrounded a tree and started barking like mad. I looked up and thought I was hallucinating: monkeys, lounging around in the branches, looking down with round, insolent eyes. One dropped down in front of us—swinging by one arm it was, right in my face. My dogs jumped up snapping but it just swung away, chattering and laughing."

'Elsewhere, battery hens in Pontypridd went on strike, refusing to lay eggs. Donkeys on a Blackpool beach formed a circle and kicked up clouds of sand, causing rides to be abandoned for the day. And perhaps strangest of all were the dozens of children taken to casualty today with their pet hamsters clamped firmly to their fingers.

'An animal behaviourist was mystified. "The whole world is unsettled," she said, "maybe the animals feel it too." '

Odd. All very odd. Animals with attitude, and it was an attitude I thought I recognised.

Next day was Saturday. I like Saturday because Charlie's usually around and it's often a gardening day. That Saturday was extra good because it was also manure day. Fortunately the pigs were still behaving like pigs, doing what they do best, in my eyes: producing lots of lovely manure.

Humans have to work for food. It doesn't come in on a sunray or rise through their veins from the soil, and because there was no oil, the food cost a lot to move around so people started growing their own. Nearly all the gardens had vegetables, many had chickens, and Brigid had pigs.

Eva swaps some of her veg for pigs' manure every few months. On a manure day we can all smell it coming, I feel my roots spreading in anticipation. Eva comes along the alley and through the gate with a great, heaped, steaming barrowload of the stuff. Did anything ever smell so divine? The scent hangs in warm folds: rich, sweet and earthy. How humans resist it I don't know. You would think they'd pile their plates high with it, but they give it all to us and treat themselves with little squares of hard brown stuff: chocolate.

I think that at some time in human history they knew better because of the saying 'manna from heaven' which means delightful food stuff falling from the skies, clearly a corruption of 'manure from heaven' which does fall on us plants from above.

I must admit that most of the manure goes to the

veg, but Charlie always brings a forkful up to me. This makes Eva smile: 'You and that tree she says, anyone would think it was a pet. Do you know that most people would chop it down. It's too close to the house; the roots could damage the foundations.'

Eva can be a little insensitive at times. There is no way I would damage the house. I'm very careful with my roots. Charlie came to stand by me like a little guard.

'You sound like Sperrin,' he said.

Eva laughed, 'Okay, I'm sorry, tree,' she said, bowing to me, 'no offence intended.'

'None taken,' I said, and Charlie giggled.

'Speaking of Mr S, I think I'd better go down and inspect the damage.'

Charlie ran off ahead and I stuck with his mind the best I could. As he neared the border I could feel the sick stupor of the smaller plants as they struggled for life. Charlie stepped over the tangle of broken branches under the old wall and started clearing them aside urgently.

'Dead, dead, dead,' he said.

'What are?' Eva asked.

'All the plants on the wall. There were fourteen species and *Junglus slaterii*.'

'What's that?'

'A rare plant I was specially looking after.'

He ran to the corner of the wall and pushed some ferns aside. 'This one's okay I think, and I've got seeds. I'll have to try and raise them all again.'

Eva glared over the fence. Sperrin was going round

his house, slamming all the windows shut. Then he came outside, and, with a handkerchief over his nose and mouth, set two big fans whirring on his patio. Seeing Eva boldly staring him down, he made to go back into the house, but changed his mind and marched purposefully over.

'I suppose this is you,' he said, letting his handkerchief down far enough to speak, then clamping it back over his nose.

'What are you talking about?' asked Eva.

'I suppose this is you again; this vile stink.'

Eva's eyes had started to sparkle. She couldn't help it, she lifted her arm and sniffed her armpit. 'No, I'm not getting anything,' she said and she looked at Charlie for confirmation. He shrugged.

'You know what I'm talking about—this dreadful mess you will keep spreading on your garden. It belongs in a farmyard not in residential areas; there should be by-laws against it. We are not medieval peasants living among pig sties.'

Up went the handkerchief again.

Eva looked into Sperrin's eyes: 'Speak for yourself,' she said, and laughed in his face.

'Oh you've got nothing to laugh about, Mrs Slater, I can assure you.'

'Oh please,' said Eva, 'you can't intimidate me,' and she turned to walk away.

Charlie followed her but felt his eyes drawn back. Sperrin was staring after them, and once again he flashed Charlie that look of undisguised malice.

'Was that childish of me? Would you say that was childish of me?' Eva asked as the two of them broke out of the orchard.

'Yes,' said Charlie. 'What did he call us?'

'Medieval peasants.' Eva grabbed Charlie and swung him around: 'The old misery is quite right, we're the new peasants and we like it.'

'And we like pigs,' chanted Charlie.

'And sties,' said Eva.

'And we lu-urve manure,' Charlie sang defiantly.

'Here, here,' the entire garden rustled.

12

Three Spies and Two Guys

For once, Charlie beat Eva to the post. He handed her a red envelope. It looked like a greetings card. Eva held it suspiciously; it was nowhere near her birthday.

'Sorry you're leaving,' the card said above a cartoon of people standing round a computer weeping very large tears. Inside was scrawled NOT.

'Sperrin?' Charlie said.

'Who else?'

'He can't sack you, can he?'

'No, but he's very friendly with people who can.' She folded her lips and shook her head. 'He's not going to beat me.'

It was easy for Eva to say that, but from where I was standing it looked like Sperrin had all the power. My imagination was getting better all the time, and, like Charlie said, if you can imagine you can worry. So I did. Vividly. And at length. What if Eva did lose her job? What if they had to sell up and move, and someone else moved in? What if Sperrin, to be certain of getting the Jungle, bought everything, me included. 'Most people would chop it down,' Eva's words echoed up and down my trunk. I could almost hear the whine of the saw, the long crack as I keeled over and the rustle as my fallen branches settled round the broken treehouse.

But worse than this was the fear that I would never see Charlie again. I needed advice. Where was Wilfred when you needed him? It was weeks since I'd seen him. I watched Charlie and Eva leave and fell to moping.

It was a greezy day (low grey sky, everything greased with a mist that wasn't quite rain). Hilda and Gilda were deep in straw, popping out their warm globes; the garden lay in long quietness.

The magpies arrived one by one until there were four strangers sitting in the shelter of my branches, monochrome like the day, but for a blue sheen on their backs. As they were newcomers I paid them some attention. They were very large for magpies; heavy as gulls, they felt. They sat up high above the treehouse. One of them, deliberately I thought, let out a dropping which fell on Charlie's notebook. Gradually I became aware of a power and a wisdom descending around me in veils. The birds hopped around, changing positions, then I looked at their eyes: great, dark, spacious things, and I knew them.

'You're the, er…the birds with the family gnosis.'

The largest magpie replied: 'We are they. Know of you. The rat has told. We seek him now.'

'I haven't seen him in a long time; it must be five weeks,' I said, running through the number of *Brooke Farms* since I last saw him. 'He said that he was going on one of his trips.'

'Coming to council. He was not there.'

Then their thoughts started to flurry and flap, zagging from one to the other. These are the bits I understood:

'No, no—I see him underground.'

'He waits to heal.'

'The smell of blood is on him. Shadows above.'

'He suffers.'

By then I was seriously agitated.

'Blood, suffering; what are you talking about?'

They all aimed the black points of their beaks at my trunk and the dark net of their calm drifted down on me. 'First know this,' they said, and they let me into their world.

Oh, what I saw. I know the mind of man; this was like the dreams of man, because I flew. The freedom, and then the sights: I've seen the ocean on TV of course, but the real ocean is terrifying in its mile-beyond-mile, swallowing vastness and it sways like one great skirt with a planetary power. And I saw trees which stretch like seas. These immense forests drew me; the song of life from them was like a billion bees humming in layers of harmony. And I saw mountains and the cities of men made small, and new rivers which only birds know, rivers of force, of magnetism which they can follow like highways from one land to another. Then came the message:

The garden flattened around me as though a tornado had passed, it opened out into a white vastness; the whiteness was ice. There were great movements and cracking in the ice, blue rumblings and now it comes, now it comes like damp-crusted sugar into deep blue tea and the tea cup overflows into the saucer and then over the table and it keeps on coming and overflowing and there's a horrid mess.

And from these great symbolic thoughts I returned to my own small ones which were a kind of helpless desire to mop up the mess. The magpies launched themselves above me, I felt a warmth from the underside of their wings and then they disappeared into the North.

I forgot about the greezy day then and mulled over the sights I had seen. If these were the things that Wilfred knew, no wonder he mocked me and my small interests. But where was Wilfred? The Pica had seen him in some sort of danger.

Surely Wilfred could get out of any spot.

I spent the rest of the day worrying alternately about Wilfred and Charlie. By the time Charlie got home, I had persuaded myself that Wilfred was dead and that the 'For Sale' sign was already up in front of the house.

Charlie came straight up, and rummaged in his scran box for an apple.

'We've got to stop it,' I said straight away.

'What?' he said, with a cheek full of apple.

'The sale.'

'What?'

'I've seen it. The house gets sold. Sperrin buys it. You go away forever. I get chopped down.'

'Calm down,' crunch, 'I'm not going to let it happen. Information is power, and that's what I'm going to get.'

He took one of his scale plans of the garden and tacked a plan of Sperrin's land to the bottom. I watched as he drew in a dotted red path which followed the wooden steps through the orchard, moseyed down through the Jungle, climbed Sycamore, dropped over Sperrin's wire fence, rolled down his bank, drew breath behind his garage, made a low run across his carpet lawn and stopped outside his kitchen window in full view of anyone looking out, and then—then the little red dashes went into the house. Oh no, what had I started?

At least the news that night reassured me:

'Reports are just coming in of turkeys flying at a Norfolk farmer and disabling him. A vet who examined one of the injured birds, had this to say:

' "The domestic turkey is a flightless bird, yet these birds somehow managed to stay in the air for several seconds. If you look at the muscles on this turkey you'd swear it had been in training. Most peculiar." '

I made a hopeful guess at the identity of the trainer. The next night I was sure.

'An army of rats attacked a bakery at Sawton Mill in Wiltshire. An estimated four thousand poured into the building spoiling several tons of flour, bread and cakes. One shocked worker said that the attack was spearheaded by a different animal—yes, it's those hamsters again.'

But Charlie's plans remained a worry. I had never seen an aura as dark as Sperrin's on any plant or animal. You may not know this but air is not dead, neither is rock nor earth. Sperrin's aura sucked the life sparkle from the air around him; it smoked out from him as from a dirty chimney. I had to stop Charlie from carrying out his spying mission. The only way I could think of to do this was to recruit some spies of my own.

I set the border trees on twenty-four hour watch and they reported some strange goings-on. First were the cracks of light seen at Sperrin's windows long after the rest of the town was folded into darkness and sleep. Odder than this was the figure seen creeping around Sperrin's garden. The man tried the doors of the outbuildings and shone a torch through the windows. Probably a burglar I thought. This was something but it wasn't enough.

Next I asked for Morwen's help. Morwen owes Charlie a favour.

When the treehouse was first built she was very upset. She had four chicks at the time and, although her nest was well up in my higher branches, she was suspicious of Charlie and his treehouse. At night she would tire herself out, spitefully pulling bits off it. Then disaster happened: one of her chicks fell out of the nest.

Now I am very fond of birds, especially the young ones. They bring out my nurturing side. During the breeding season I love to chick-sit while the parents are off hunting for food. Picture this: let your eyes get used to the shade and have a look; you can just make out their funny yellow clown-mouths and scrawny necks. Not pretty, till the feathers come, but their mothers love them.

Why then, don't birds build the sides of the nest higher? When chicks topple out I do my best to break the fall but mostly it's no use. It's a sad thing to see the little blind and naked birds littering the ground. I have suggested to Morwen that she build her nest higher. She cocks her head, agrees vaguely, then makes her nest the way she always has.

On this occasion Morwen's chick was saved by Charlie's cushion on the treehouse platform, only to face a greater danger. I had just tuned in to a terrible conversation between Adolf and his friend Zak. The cats were saying how they love a chick, light and fluffy on the outside with a crunch in the middle.

Believe it. Then Adolf started to pad towards me. He put a testing paw up against my trunk and unsheathed his claws.

One of my tricks for teaching imagination is this: I get the student plant to imagine the sun twice as big and twice as strong as it really is, and shining from a different direction. If they do it well they can make their leaves or branches move towards the imaginary sun. This is because plants always grow towards the light. I practised this myself until I could move my branches at will—slowly, it's true, but I was getting better at it.

I felt Adolf leap and knew that I had to act quickly. I imagined the strongest, whitest, light of twenty suns, streaming from the heart of the nestling. It worked. My branches swung and drew close about the tiny chick; a spray of leaves lay gently over it.

Cats bother me; they only have two ways of being. They ripple around the garden, or bask in the best spot, so laid back they're falling off the horizon, yet full of controlled menace; or there's the fully alert state, every nerve a needle; 'get ready to die,' they are saying, and mostly it happens just like that.

With one scrabbling leap Adolf was on the treehouse platform with his nose in the air, letting the smell of nestling stream by his nostrils. I bashed a branch against Charlie's bedroom window and 'shouted' to him in shrill panic. Charlie looked up and dived down the chute at the same time as Morwen arrived back with a beak full of grubs. She saw three where there had been four, dropped the grubs on their heads, took in the cat and Charlie below, and flapped frantically down on them both. Charlie shooed Adolf away. Adolf stood his ground, stared coolly as if to say 'I'll be back', then bounded unhurriedly downwards.

Charlie was on his knees asking, 'Where is it, Ash?' while Morwen continued flapping hysterically at his head.

'On the cushion,' I told him, swishing my leaves aside.

He lifted the cushion carefully. The chick kept gaping around as though it was still in the nest.

I shouted at Morwen, 'Calm down now. He won't hurt it.'

'It's all right,' Charlie said to Morwen, 'it's all safe,' and he climbed up where I had to brace myself to support him, and returned the little bird to safety.

So Morwen owed Charlie a favour. Living so close to me and scoffing hundreds of my berries every summer, she had soaked up some gnosis over the years; still it wasn't easy to get across what I wanted her to do. I didn't want her to take any risks with Adolf and Zak around but I asked her if she could get a look through Sperrin's windows. Could she spot anything unusual?

Morwen has every reason to dislike Sperrin. Her clan's territory was cleared to make room for his house, leaving many homeless, so she wanted to help, but she's a nervy type and has a special fear of Adolf. However, she did her best and reported back.

'Looks like any other house to me,' she said, 'there are square spaces inside, full of mostly dead things.'

'That's furniture,' I said patiently; 'think carefully, did you see anything else?'

'Only when I landed on the kitchen windowsill.' She puffed out her feathers and withdrew her head into them as though she wanted to hide. 'He was bending to his food and I must have caught his eye because he lifted his head and looked straight at me with those yellow lamps. I froze and he came bursting out of the hole in the door.'

'You mean Adolf,' I said; 'he came out through the cat flap.'

She nodded. 'I can't go back.'

'No, no. Of course not, Morwen, but thanks.'

I needed a better, bolder observer to spy for me, someone who was used to human ways, who might spot if something was out of the ordinary.

Something made me turn towards the vegetable plot where a cabbage leaf appeared to walk by itself up the garden. As it came towards me I saw that the holes in its leaves glinted and that it had a tail.

'Wilfred!' I called happily. 'You're alive.'

'Of course I'm alive, whatever made you think otherwise?'

He dropped the leaf but still stood cautiously close to cover. I told him about the visit of the magpies and what they had seen.

'Oh yes the Pica, Pica sapiens. It's true what they saw; I did allow myself to get into some difficulties. Men can't trick me with traps and poisons; I've long been wise to all that. My own pride caught me out this time. You'd think I'd know better at my age. I was flushed with the success of my latest venture. It's the first mass protest I've managed to organise. More and more animals are coming on board. My cousins, the hamsters, are very keen. You can always rely on the rodents: small bodies but hearts like lions.'

'All that on the news, about animals behaving oddly—that was all your doing?'

'Let's say I sowed the seed. I've grown impatient with the council—decided to branch out on my own, whip up a bit of action. Anyway, as I said, my success made me bold; I stopped hiding, thought I was invulnerable and got whopped with a garden spade—broke a few bones, but I lay low, ate the right roots and it's all mended. What else did the Pica want? They didn't come just to tell you about my little mishap, did they?'

I showed him the Pica's message and he pondered long on it, his eyes rolling trance-like.

'What's it about?' I asked.

'The last piece, the trigger. Now it will roll on till the end,' he murmured as he came out of his trance. Certain now that it was all beyond me, I asked no more questions. I had other problems to deal with. I put into practice something I had learned from *Brooke Farm*—deviousness.

'I wanted to ask you a favour,' I said, 'but I can see it's not a good time. You'll be feeling nervous around humans for a while yet.'

'Nervous,' he laughed. 'Not me—I just forgot my common sense. Humans are slow but they're also big and strong and they often have weapons to hand. But I have no fear of them.'

Then with the world's worst timing Charlie came out of the house.

'Hello little fella, would you like a crisp?'

Charlie was leaning towards Wilfred, holding out a cone of home-made crisps wrapped in bread paper.

Wilfred seemed to think he was still in a trance state. Slowly it dawned on him that it was a real human in front of him. Usually when humans see Wilfred they scream. What they never do is offer him a crisp. Wilfred was confused, befuddled and as he looked into Charlie's leaf-lit green eyes, almost charmed. Then all his prejudices came back, he ran at Charlie and attacked his shoe. Charlie watched him without fear. He stretched his leg out and Wilfred dangled foolishly from his shoe lace. Charlie laughed and Wilfred scampered off in a huff. I watched his tail snake through the hedge and looked forward to our next meeting.

Charlie climbed up to the treehouse eating his crisps and got out his plans again. I jumped in and told him all I knew.

'It's worth investigating further then.'

'No, no; not worth it at all. That's all there is; there's nothing else to see. All the trees down there have been watching for weeks, and let me tell you, if there's one thing trees are good at, it's watching.'

'I just want to see for myself. There might be some clues they missed.'

'Doubt it, doubt it very much.'

'Ash, I can read you like a book; there's nothing to worry about. I just want to see for myself, all right?'

And off he went. Every night he went down to the fence, climbed Sycamore, watched and scribbled notes.

After a week of this he took his notebook into the house and reported to Eva what he'd seen.

> Monday 7:14 p.m.—Sperrin leaves house with big envelope. Returns 7:39.
>
> Tuesday 8:06 p.m.: power cut. Lights stay on.

Thursday 6:15 p.m.—man comes to house, doesn't look friendly. Sperrin swaps something on doorstep, tells him *not to come to house again in daylight*.

Charlie emphasized this last point slowly.

Friday: Sperrin using floodlights to trim his soldiers.

Saturday: 11.47 a.m. Sperrin tells his wife off because she hasn't folded the rotary washing line away. 12.05 p.m.: Sperrin calls his wife again—'Oona, come and take a letter'—just like she's his secretary.

'She used to be,' said Eva.

'To sum up: doorstep dealings—possibly dodgy; lights on in a power cut; reckless energy use.'

'Not really much to go on, love.'

Charlie chewed his pencil. 'It points though; it points to…something. Any more hassle at work?'

'I haven't seen Sperrin this week; he's leaving me alone pretty much.'

Charlie looked up into Eva's face. 'And?'

'How do you do that? Okay—Jules, his secretary, gave me a warning: 'I'm not mentioning any names,' she said, 'but watch your back.'

'You need to get friendly; groom her, get her to grass.'

'Hold on, where did grass come into this?' I interrupted. I do hate to lose the thread of a story.

Through the window Charlie rolled his eyes at me.

A few days later Charlie went to Eva again.

'It's all coming together,' he said mysteriously. 'Guess what the Sperrins have got in their second garage?'

'Don't tell me, a machine for mashing up kids.'

'Ha-ha. Actually, it's a generator. And—he takes his gas guzzler to work every day.'

'No he doesn't. The car park's practically empty. I'd notice if his car was there every day. He might take it in once or twice a month, but that's no more than some others.'

'He parks in the side streets using different spots. Now why would he do that?'

'I can't imagine.'

'Also, he clocked 328 miles last weekend.'

'How do you know all this? I've told you not to go near Sperrin.'

'I didn't. It was one of my associates.'

'You've got associates. Who?'

'I'm not allowed to say.'

It was fortunate for Charlie that just then, the phone rang. But he still had me to answer to.

'Like to put names to your associates?' I said, trying to sound strict and teacherish.

'There's only one actually. Let's just call him "the burglar".'

13

My History

I had never known Charlie to give up on anything. I could think of only one way to put him off Sperrin's trail and that was to give him a new interest.

The answer came to me as I noticed a seedling of Holly's, not much more than a twig in the ground with perfect spiny leaves. I tried to remember when I was the same size, and I fell to wondering about my parent tree and my grandparent.

'Who am I?' I murmured listlessly.

'What did you say, Ash?'

'Who am I really? Where did I come from?'

'Well, your seeds are spread by birds. They eat your berries; the berries pass through their digestive system and get spread in their droppings, sometimes miles from the parent tree.'

'You humans are lucky. You've got so much history, so many stories. I've got weather history of course, but I'd like some stories of my own.'

And that was all it took. You have to be careful about asking Charlie a question, because he can never rest until he's answered it, and answered it thoroughly.

For several weeks Charlie disappeared into town every Saturday morning. He went to the library, and he also attended some lectures on 'The Wisdom of Trees' at a place called the Rainbow Café, which sounded fascinating. It turns out that my family was once very important and famous.

'The Mountain Ash or Rowan,' Charlie said, 'in winter, when frosted like stars, was topped by the pagans with a special star. The star-clad Rowan was the first Christmas tree. It stood for light returning to the world of darkness.'

Wow, I hadn't been expecting anything like that. Star-clad trees. I imagined my ancestors gracing ancient hillsides at the dawn of the world, glittering with frost, and some pagan child, a child like Charlie, fixing his own star to the tree with wonder in his green eyes.

'Your berries heal, protect and give long life,' he went on, 'and here it says your red berries and green leaves inspired Scottish tartan.'

That was just the start; there were many more tales of magic and mystery. There was a terrible battle between an eagle and demons, and wherever a feather or a drop of blood fell to earth, a Rowan grew. That's why we have red berries and feathery leaves. I also have an ancestor who saved the god Thor from drowning.

The stories were wonderful but what I really appreciated was the respect we once had. 'I think,' I said, 'that trees were important to people once. But now, they don't see us any more do they, not really?'

'I see you, Ash,' Charlie said.

After one of his trips to the library he asked, 'Would you mind if I borrowed some of your twigs?'

'Go ahead.'

He snapped off two twigs, and taking some red wool from his pocket, bound the twigs together into a cross.

'It's a Rowan cross—' he explained, '—used for protection.'

My plan had worked far better than I had hoped. Perhaps when he was done with Rowans he would start on the histories of the other trees. I thought I was getting pretty skilled at handling humans, and foolishly, I relaxed.

Christmas came, and there was light. Well before dawn the windows started to glow. Little beacons shone wherever there were children. The government had said there would be cheap power for a full twenty-four hours. Steam drifted from heating vents.

Charlie's present was an old book that Eva had unearthed at a garden sale: *Field and Forest Lore*. It was so old that the words and spellings came from another time. Charlie couldn't have been more pleased.

'It's full of forgotten knowledge,' he said, 'and look at this picture.'

'*Junglus slaterii*.'

'Yes. Inktop it was called. For liver complaints. Purifies the blood. Thank goodness I saved it.'

Charlie studied every page of the book and spent the darkest days of January adding to his notes.

After a humid, cloying winter with barely a frost, the garden was confused. We looked to the weather as conductor, but she would jab with her baton one day and the next let her arm trail listlessly. I said we should go by the calendar but only a few were strong enough to stay with me. The rest were dragged into bud and flower far too early. Spring was sucked out of us unearned by hardship and chills.

The post had been interrupted for weeks because of a new crisis in petrol supplies. It had started up again but there was only one delivery per week.

Charlie brought a pile of letters into the kitchen and placed it silently on the table in front of Eva. Bills of course, plus one other letter. They both knew what it was. Eva sighed and opened it resignedly. Her eyes skimmed it, then she read in a dead-sounding voice: 'New Year is a time for resolutions. Want to know mine? Learn it from the pantomime—look out he's behind you.'

Charlie picked up the card and studied it closely. He ran the card absently under his nose and looked puzzled. As he turned the envelope over something fell onto the table.

Eva jumped up and screamed her fingers spread out stiffly. 'Oh God, what is that?'

Charlie held it up. It swung horribly in his fingers. 'I think it's a… it looks like a rat's tail.'

'He's unhinged,' Eva said. 'You'd better not go anywhere alone for a while.'

'He doesn't scare me.'

'Better be on the safe side.'

Later that day my spirits sank as Charlie got out his spying plan and traced over the little red dashes with a pencil. It was time to speak to Wilfred again. I knew he wouldn't do anything to help humans. I would have to offer him something in return. To my relief, he arrived on cue, complete with tail, and I prepared to bargain.

'Find out what's going on down there and I promise I'll pay you back. I'll do anything you ask so long as no one is harmed by it.'

His paws moved over his nose in an automatic washing motion, not quite hiding a wily grin.

'Done,' he said, pressing a cool paw against my trunk by way of sealing the bargain. 'Life's been quiet lately, I could use a bit of adventure to keep me sharp, a bit of stim-u-lation.'

'Wilfred,' I said, as he trotted off, 'be careful.'

'This is no more than a stroll in the sewer to me,' he scoffed.

And that was the last I saw of him. For two days and nights I waited. I quizzed the border trees. I grilled Morwen, but it was the third night before news reached me.

Night-time in the garden is a whole different world. A new cast of characters comes on: hedgehog, fox, bat, a steady stream of cats passing through. The plants, though, are resting. Flowers close, leaves fold and instead of closing my eyes I close my stomata, the little holes on the undersides of my leaves. I drift in and out of rest, catch glimpses of what's going on: a cat taking a shrew, and so on; I might join a wakeful group of plants chatting quietly together before I drift off again. I'd recently begun getting open, floaty feelings as though my roots were not in the ground but in the air. Charlie said it was a sign that I would start dreaming soon. At first that's what I thought it was.

'I've finally got that smug old rat where I want him,' Adolf was saying to Zak. 'I caught the whiff of him, followed his trail to the office and got there just in time to see him slip inside the safe. My homer stuffed some papers in there and locked him in. I've slipped out while they're asleep but I'll be back on watch in the morning. I want to be there when he's found,' he licked his black lips unhurriedly. 'He's probably starved or suffocated by now, but the body should still come my way.'

I checked my roots. The heavy earth held them snug, so I knew it was no dream.

What could I do? Wilfred was in deep trouble and it was my fault. I couldn't ask Charlie for help. I'd started all this to keep him out of danger in the first place.

But an hour later Charlie took matters out of my hands.

He slid down the chute and crawled out onto the platform. He was dressed all in black and his face was smeared with dirt. There was a look on his face I'd never seen there before: hard and determined, and he seemed to be ignoring me. He dropped quietly to the ground. Only then did he glance up at me.

'Don't worry,' he said, 'there's something I have to do.' His bobbing torch moved towards the Jungle.

'Wait,' I called after him, and I told him about Wilfred.

'Well, that complicates things. But I'll save him if I can.'

'No, wait—it's not worth it.' I was finding out where my loyalty lay.

'I'll be careful.'

'Famous last words,' I said, and Charlie turned round and smiled as he always does when I use a line from *Brooke Farm* without really understanding what it means.

But I was serious about the last words. It was madness. Anyone would think he'd never watched TV. He would certainly be taken hostage and there would be a police shoot-out; someone would end up in a coma and I hoped it wouldn't be Charlie.

'Stop!' I tried again, but the torch kept bobbing along. 'It might be better if you did leave,' I said desperately. 'Sell up. You'll find another garden.'

Charlie stopped. The torchlight dropped in an arc to his side; his head dropped forward, and he turned slowly.

'Just like that. Just leave. Find another garden.' He shook his head. 'You don't give up on what you lo…' He swallowed hard. 'This is it. There is no other garden.'

And he pushed on into the trees at a run. He knew

the arrangement of every tangle, root and bramble in the Jungle; even so, at that pace he would surely trip or crash into something. A few more flickers of the torch and he was gone. I tried to tune to him and he let me in just long enough to show me a cold, determined energy before he slammed the door of his mind and shut me out.

'I'm sorry,' I signalled. 'I didn't mean that.'

But my words bounced back from a dumb, blank wall. Like ivy I crept around it trying for crevices. There was nothing. For the first time since my awakening I had no sense of Charlie's existence. He was dead to me.

It was then that I realised the difference between watching a drama from the outside (fun), watching it from the inside (hairy), and being inside and helpless (horrible).

Desolate, I tuned to the border trees. Sycamore was the first to pick up.

'What's with you?' he asked. 'You sound like you've been stripped by grubs. Hold on, what's that light?'

'Charlie's on his way down there. I need you to watch him and tell me what's going on.'

'I see him, he's headed this way and now he's…' Sycamore's signal dipped. '…He's starting to climb me. He's edging along one of my branches on the border side; he's right at the edge of my branch, the one that Sperrin lopped. Now he's swinging out, he's flying over the fence.'

Sycamore fell silent.

'What's he doing now?'

'I don't know—there was a thud.'
'And?'
'I've got him. He's crouching beside that new building.'
'Is he hidden?'
'Only by darkness.'

There followed a long wait while Charlie remained where he was. Sycamore could tell me nothing else in spite of my nervous badgering. The moon moved another fraction across the sky and I heard the growing drone of a car, unusual at night. The car stopped somewhere close by and a door banged threateningly.

'Sperrin's got visitors,' Sycamore said, 'two men. They're carrying things up the drive, round things, like tree trunks, and stacking them by the garage. Sperrin's coming out with keys. Charlie's heading for the bushes. If any of them look this way they must see him.'

Just then Charlie thought of me. I slipped back into his head as torchlight flicked across him. He was standing motionless in a line of topiary soldiers, doing his best to think and look like a tree. Sperrin was only feet away, training the torchlight on the head of each soldier in turn. Charlie screwed his eyes up as though waiting for a blow. All his attention went to his hand which held a little wooden cross bound with red thread. The beam passed down the line, reaching the soldier right next to Charlie.

'Rustle!' I shouted at the border trees, and again: 'Rustle!'

A wave of rustling passed along the border, as though

a very large animal was coming through. Sperrin swung the torch around the tree-tops surprising a trapezing dormouse.

'Jumpy tonight, Gov,' said one of the men.

'Keep your voice down, will you,' hissed Sperrin, sorting through his keys. Then the large double doors swung out, hiding Charlie from view.

Across the lawn the door of the house was still slightly open, and Charlie, utterly reckless, was running towards it. If I had a heart it would have had an attack. He stood in the hallway panting. The lights dazzled him, used as he was to dim bulbs and candles.

'I'll take six more barrels this week. Wait here and I'll get the necessary.' It was Sperrin coming in.

Charlie ducked into the room on the right. It was a small office with a desk piled with slips of paper in bundles, some filing cabinets and a safe. Charlie slid between the filing cabinet and the window.

The men became involved in a long conversation about money; they wanted more and Sperrin didn't want to give it to them. At last they reached a deal.

'I'll give you thirty extra for each barrel, but I want those vouchers shifting by next week.'

'No probs, Guv. We've got customers waiting.'

Sperrin moved towards the safe. There was a series of whirrs and clicks, the door swung open and Sperrin reached inside. Wilfred nipped. Sperrin stepped back swearing, unable to believe what he was seeing. There was Wilfred, lounging in the greatest comfort on a perfectly round nest of shredded bank notes. Wilfred enjoyed the moment for as long as he dared, then leapt out and away, but he hadn't reckoned on the effects of hunger and the lack of air. He staggered groggily. Adolf was ready. He gathered himself to pounce, twitching his haunches for perfect poise and alignment before rushing his kill. Charlie threw himself across the room and Wilfred scuttled for the door. Chaos followed.

In the hall, Sperrin grabbed an umbrella, lunged at Wilfred, missed and crunched Adolf on the curve of his spine. Adolf yowled, turned and swiped at Sperrin's shins with his devilish claws. Wilfred hurtled through the cat flap with Adolf close behind. Charlie made his own run for the door but Sperrin dragged him back by the collar.

'The Slater brat, isn't it? Come thieving, have you? Did she send you? Getting desperate for money now, is she? Let's take you home and see what she has to say.'

Outside the men dashed about the floodlit garden after Wilfred, while Oona came quietly up behind Charlie and did a very strange thing. She slipped something into his hand. Charlie looked over his shoulder at her, then moved his hand stealthily to his pocket.

'Give it up,' Sperrin called angrily to the men. 'Give it up and get out of here. I've got other business to attend to now.'

I felt an indignant paw on my trunk. 'Wake up, will you, I said good evening.'

'Wilfred, are you all right? What about Charlie?'

'Being bundled into a car about now, I should think. Sperrin's bringing him home.'

Eva kept Sperrin at the front door. I couldn't tune to Charlie; he was too wretched. I could just catch the rise and fall of voices, then the slamming of the door. Eva's face was tight with anger as she pushed Charlie into his room, locked the chute and hid the key. I could have told him exactly where she put it. But for once I was with Eva.

Charlie sat on the bed with his torch, head hanging. 'Well, let's see what this is about,' he sighed, emptying his pocket. 'Petrol vouchers. That's what I thought. Sperrin is head of the environment dept at the council. They issue these, so Sperrin must be stealing them and using them to get petrol for himself; it also seems like he sells them for cash through these men. I expect he'll be sacked for this. He might even go to jail. Mum will come round when I tell her.'

But she didn't. Not for days. She was still shaken and very cross.

'Promise you'll never do anything so silly again. Don't even go near the fence. You don't know how risky that was. He's a very bad man.'

'But it wasn't…'

'I don't want to hear it—I thought I could trust you. It's half my fault, I know. I confide in you too much, then you take it on yourself to solve my problems. Still you mustn't take things so far.'

Charlie stomped out of the house, looking for sympathy, but I had to tell him that I agreed with Eva.

'You shouldn't have done it,' I said, 'it was too risky.'

'Look,' he said, 'I'm not stupid. I did my homework first—trust me.'

But I carried on nagging; I couldn't let it drop. Even to myself I sounded like Sally Durrell, the nag of the North.

'I had allies,' he said at last, 'here, let me show you.'

14

Strange Allies

And he opened his memory. Just as I'd shown him what the rings in my trunk held, he took me back a few months.

'Watch.'

I found myself, or rather Charlie's self, on the High Street. On either side of him white-washed windows and closing-down signs. At the fruit shop he swerved out into the road where reaching and grabbing bodies pressed around a stand of bananas. The shoppers looked like hunters. From the old TV shows I'd seen, I knew that things used to be different. Shoppers then swung glossy carriers and their faces had a spoilt, come-on-tickle-my-fancy look. Charlie walked past Radeby's, a big department store. Its windows were dusty with old stock. A naked dummy lay on its side; dead flies lay on their backs. He made for the one spot of colour on the High Street: the Rainbow Café. It sat in its own glow. Underneath the outdoor tables lush grass grew through cracks in the pavement.

Charlie found a small table under the notice board. He pretended to read some very commendable leaflets about hugging trees while he waited for the cheapest thing on the menu, watery squash.

A woman leaned over Charlie. 'Sorry,' she said, 'excuse me a minute,' and she scribbled down the date of a lecture: 'Towards a Simpler Life'.

Charlie looked up from behind his menu.

'Hello Mrs Sperrin,' he said tentatively.

'Hello,' she said, her face leaping into a smile. 'It's Charlie, isn't it?' There was a well-meaning pause. 'I'm just having another drink. Can I get you one?' What have you got there—squash? We can do better than that,' and she ordered hot chocolate with marshmallows and cream and chocolate curls.

I felt Charlie sink in warm chocolate bubbles. He watched Oona lick a line of froth from under her nose and knew that he could trust her.

They talked politely for a few minutes, then Oona put her head on one side and gave Charlie a very searching look.

'Funny how you seem very old and very young at the same time,' she said, and then she started to talk. She was like a fizzy drink shaken up.

'You do understand?' she kept saying. Charlie nodded and that was all she needed.

'I thought that boys gave you headaches.'

'Who told you that?'

'Mr Sperrin.'

'Charlie, it's Mr Sperrin who gives me a headache. Oh!' she covered her mouth. 'I can't believe I just said that. Well I've said it now,' and she laughed with a kind of relief. 'Somehow you make me honest.'

The wall clock whizzed round. Oona ordered custard slices.

'The world's in a mess Charlie—' custard oozed messily down Charlie's hand '—and there are people, even on sinking ships, who try to gain some advantage over the rest. Do you understand me? They think they're clever; they think they're in control, but they're little people, Charlie, and I'm sorry for what he's done, sorry that I ever went along with it. The letters were the worst...oh, I mean, well I'd better not say any more.'

I was confused. 'Is she speaking in code? Can you rewind that bit?'

'You have to learn to read between the lines, Ash. I'll just tell you the rest. We met up at the café a few more times. Oona wanted to know more about us and how we were managing to live.'

'I hope you didn't give anything away; she could be a double agent.'

'No, Ash, I did what you taught me to do. I checked her aura. It's shell pink, and a bit timid, as though she's afraid to glow, but it's constant. It doesn't waver and wobble like a liar's. And you know the mystery gift we got in the post, the bundle of notes, I didn't tell Mum, but the scent that came out of the envelope, a smell like clean washing, that's the scent of Oona's clothes.

Sperrin made her type all those letters but she hated doing it. That's why she sent us the money. And that's why I risked going into the house. She wouldn't have let him hurt me.'

'So she was your "associate"?'

'And Graham. He was the "burglar" doing a bit of spying of his own.'

'Why would he do that?'

'Because he cares about…us. He shadowed Sperrin's car as well. Then there's your pal the rat. He's awesome, isn't he? So you see, it wasn't as risky as it seemed. I knew there was help if things got really sticky—and I had this.'

He took the Rowan cross out of his pocket, held it up and chanted, "Rowan Ash and red thread, hold the witches all in dread.' Ancient rhyme, protects from evil. It worked too. I stood in full view and they looked right through me. Now I've shown you my memories I think it's time you showed me yours. What's all this nonsense about Graham?'

'Like I said, he's hiding something.'

'What about his aura—it's gold and rock steady.'

'I know, but you haven't seen what I've seen.'

'Show me then.'

'All right you asked for it, but prepare to be shocked.'

I found the point just a few cells' thickness back from my newest growth, there was a flash of Adolf prowling around the orchard. 'Oops sorry, wrong place. Aah, here we are.' The terrible scene floated between us:

There was the poor man in the round sunglasses, a

bandanna on his head, a very long beard split into two plaits, leather trousers.

'He looks interesting,' said Charlie.

'Yes, poor thing,' I said.

Graham came at the man from behind with the drill, marking him terribly. It was worse than I remembered. But Charlie seemed untroubled. The memory ended.

'Well, is that it?' he said smiling.

'That's it,' I said, beginning to feel an unfamiliar prickling.

'Ash, Graham was giving that man a tattoo—a decoration on his skin. He won the world tattooist championships in Japan five years ago. He only tattoos friends since he started doing comics and fantasy book covers.'

The prickling was my first ever taste of embarrassment. 'Well, you seem to know a lot about Graham. I didn't realise you two were so thick.'

'The only thing Graham is hiding is how much he likes Mum, so I had to check him out.'

To me this was an exciting development. Romance is one of the more intriguing aspects of human behaviour. I knew the signs from *Brooke Farm*. It starts with eyeballing and moves on to word games. The couple drink strange potions, spray themselves with flower scents and eventually press their eating organs together—you couldn't make it up.

Sensing my excitement, Charlie looked at me with something like exasperation.

'Fickle's the word for you,' he said.

'Aren't you pleased then?' I asked.

'Charlie, come down.' It was Eva. Charlie inched over to the trapdoor on his belly and looked down. 'I know you only wanted to help,' she said. He had shown her the petrol vouchers that morning, she'd listened to his side of the story and had some time to think.

'Come up,' Charlie said.

Eva's head came through the hatch, a twig stuck in her curly hair. She leaned her elbows on the platform. 'I just don't know what to do about all this.'

'Yes, the spit's really hit the fan,' I said—cleverly, I thought.

Charlie gave a hysterical whine.

'Well, I'm glad you can laugh about it,' Eva said wonderingly.

Charlie recovered. 'You've got to report him. We can't let him get away with it.'

'No. No, we can't. I'll speak to Karen tomorrow.

'Will they give you your old job back, Mum?'

'I doubt it but I can try.'

'They're all in it, I swear,' said Eva when she got home the next day. 'Karen said she couldn't do anything without real proof. "These are serious accusations," she said. "What are a few dirty oil vouchers and the word of a little boy—an imaginative, mischievous little boy, a little boy who's allowed to go trespassing, alone in the dead of night?" She made me feel like a bitter, vengeful woman, and a bad mother. Maybe she's right.'

'Go to the police then. You can't just let him win.'

'He hasn't won though, has he? We're managing better now; we've still got the Jungle; let's just be grateful for that.'

Though Eva couldn't hear me, I offered her this bit of tree wisdom: 'The wind always turns; wait a while.'

I told Wilfred how things had turned out.

'I think,' he said, 'there's more fun to be had in those quarters,' and he sniggered rattily. Privately, I thought he had something left to prove. He couldn't leave it at that—rescued by a human. Some weeks later he brought me this tale:

'I used my network of informers to find out when Adolf was roaming some distance from home. I let myself in by the cat flap—so convenient—loitered in the kitchen, ate some delectable round things out of a box, and left my trademark circle of droppings in Adolf's dish. I padded around upstairs on the thick carpets, then settled myself in the bathroom ready for my favourite sport. The timing was perfect. I leapt out of the toilet bowl and sunk my teeth into Sperrin's behind. Bog ambush! It beats all, I tell you. He screamed, he shimmied, he rolled on the floor; but I just swung with a grip like a trap. When I was ready, I let go and galloped down the stairs leaving him to stumble over his own trousers—they always do that. I looked up, showed him the length of my teeth and left him on his knees swearing and screaming for his wife.

I could do nothing but marvel at Wilfred's audacity.

'That's called revenge, isn't it?' I mused. 'Paying back bad with bad. It's one of those human things that I never really understood. I always thought that if you fall over a tree root, say, and then in revenge you turn around and kick it, all you do is hurt your foot. But I'm beginning to see now.'

'You have a simple way of looking at things,' said Wilfred. 'Revenge can be, will be, very sweet, I believe.'

I didn't know what he was talking about but it gave me a hollow feeling in my trunk.

'What about paying back good with good,' he went on, 'does that strike you as fair?'

'Yes,' I said, 'everybody gains from that.'

'Are you ready now to pay back your old friend Wilfred for his, how did you put it just now: wit, nerve, courage; for risking my own life in fact?'

'Of course I am. That was the deal. I just can't think of anything big enough that I can do for you.'

Wilfred, of course, had no such difficulties.

15

Catch a Falling Star

'All I ask for now is that you keep an open mind,' Wilfred warned, 'but a day may come when I ask more. It's time to let you in on a few secrets. The greatest gathering of gnostics ever held will take place very soon. In a few weeks I head North for the first session. The Pica is going to read the signs gathered from every corner of the earth and she will then predict the future of the planet as closely as it can be told. After that we vote.'

'What about?' I said, beginning to feel uneasy.

'The humans. Is the planet a better place with or without them?'

'And what if the vote goes against them.'

'We have options.'

'Such as?'

He slid over my question. The council's aim, he said, was to save the planet from the humans who were destroying it. I would be on the agenda for the next meeting—how to get the plants involved.

Now all this was a lot to take in. I said that I would have to think about it all very carefully and maybe talk to some of the other plants.

Wilfred's whiskers shot upright: 'What do you mean *talk* to the other plants, you don't mean that there are more like you?'

It just slipped out. It was no good back-tracking. Wilfred was too sharp for that, so I played it down as much as I could.

'Not exactly like me; but plants are more connected than animals, not so separate. I've been teaching some of them to think. Some can't do it at all, but others are beginning to understand.'

Wilfred shut up then. I looked at his energy field and it was boiling.

'So you can pass it on,' he said. 'It's here then, the turning point is here. This puts a new twist on things. I must consult.'

He can be very dramatic. Sometimes I think he's a secret soap-watcher on the quiet. Anyway he ran off.

'Don't go anywhere,' he called back to me.

As if.

Brooke Farm's theme tune was playing and I had missed the ending.

The next night Wilfred came back and told me that I could be the Teacher they were all waiting for but I had to get serious, I *had* to give up my loyalty to Charlie. It was no good my teaching the whole garden to think if all they wanted to do then was watch TV (if a tree could blush I would have flamed like a maple in

September). Only the night before, half the garden was enthralled by Sally Durell's wedding. I have a horror that Wilfred will catch us at it some time.

'You could be one of the greats,' Wilfred interrupted my guilty thoughts, 'there is no doubt, you will be remembered and revered as first among flora.'

'I think you've got the wrong tree. There's nothing special about me.'

'Self-evidently wrong. Stand tall; say hello to your destiny. I see it all. Maybe they can manage without animals for a while, though they won't like it, but if the plants turn it's goodbye humans.'

'If they're clever enough to make TVs, I think they can manage without us,' I said.

'You don't get it, do you?' said Wilfred, amazed at my stupidity. 'Without you lot we'd all die—you, the plants, are the most important things on this planet,' and then he did a strange thing; almost involuntarily he bowed to me.

The solemn moment dissolved as he rolled on his back, mouth lolling. He stayed there for a silly length of time.

'Wilfred!'

He didn't move.

'Wilfred, wouldn't Adolf like to see that soft belly fur, and those pink pads waving in the air?'

That did it. He spun over.

'Just making a point. That's how we'd all be: every animal, humans included, would go belly up without you lot. You make the air breathable.'

'Really?'

'Yes. At dawn you're breathing out pure oxygen. The birds get high on it and they sing at a vibration which helps the plants to grow.'

'The dawn chorus.'

'That's right, a big old lovefest between the birds and the plants.'

I liked that, the greenery and the birds together, literally breathing life into every new day.

He looked at me shrewdly.

'So you see how well we work together, flora and fauna. It could all be so perfect if it weren't for…'

I started folding my leaves into myself. There was truth in what he said but I didn't want to see it. Wilfred saw me shutting down.

'All right, enough for one day; I know what you're thinking—and as humans go,' he took a deep breath, 'he's a decent kid.' He said this quickly, as if the words stung his tongue and he needed to spit them out.

I was listening again.

'But there's a lot at stake here,' he went on. 'The Pica showed you the rain forests. You, yes you, could save them. Or will you choose the boy?'

And off he went. I felt torn. For the first time I regretted my gnosis. The head of the Pica floated into my mind with these words: 'There's no going back from knowing, but there's peace at the end of the flight.'

What I needed was to go green for a while, maybe for a whole day. The sun was setting and the sky was tiered like a purple stadium; the darkening tiers melted into soft furrows, melted again into smoke pillars and drifted away. Peace.

And something else; another feeling, but as I tried to hold it, it lost its substance like the clouds.

I felt more settled then and rested deeply, only stirring when Charlie came stealthily up the ladder. Ever since Charlie's night jaunt Eva had continued locking the chute at night—for her own peace of mind she said, so Charlie came the long way round and he came equipped for activity.

He was carrying star charts and a compass. I nudged into his thoughts. He was preparing for something; something nice and exciting—a meteor shower, one of the best in years. That was good. I could use a distraction. I let the rest of the garden know. Everything stirred and we opened ourselves to the Western sky where Charlie was training his telescope. And what a show it was.

The sky at that time was properly dark. The street lights died at midnight. If there were lights to be seen they were the small soft lights of candles, so the stars could be seen for what they truly were and starlight had a meaning again. I had not seen true starlight until the first lights-out curfews. I hadn't rested for a week then. I just gazed up, so that the branches which grew towards the sun started to spread more evenly towards the stars. In a true starlit sky there are dizzying ranks beyond ranks beyond ranks of stars; intense whites, haloes of red and blue, and they twinkle like in the rhyme.

Against that curtain the meteor shower came down. The stars had started raining. Charlie threw his telescope aside and climbed as high into my branches as he could get. I did my best to lift him towards the stars and we watched together. Then, just as we thought it was over, one of the last falling lights carried on falling. It fell through space, it fell through sky, it fell through Cornwall. It was fire, a white ball with a tail of fire. My branch bent under Charlie's weight straining upward. I thought: he's doing that, he's bringing the meteor down, he wants to catch a falling star. And he held out his arms.

I was holding him, he wasn't holding on to me. The whole garden was lit with the fire. The shrews and moles and cats looked up with white blind-seeming eyes. Charlie, for heaven's sake, I thought, and the blazing rock seemed to pass right between his hands before it burrowed a full foot down into the garden. Eerie space steam rose from the hole. We all gasped and waited for the little alien to come crawling out—I was sure that it would look like a cat, but there was nothing. The steam got less and we waited for it to cool. Charlie didn't want to dowse it with water in case he washed off any magical space dust. Eventually he got impatient and fetched the fireplace tongs. Then he lay it on a piece of foil and brought it up into the tree to cool. The sky was lightening in the East, so Charlie slipped back indoors and I was left alone with the space rock.

I had a spooky feeling running just under my bark, as though I was being watched. I looked around the garden just greying in the dawn. Three sets of black eyes were trained on Charlie's bedroom window. Two magpies were posted in the apple trees at each edge of the garden; one sat higher in a fir. My thoughts went out to them questioning, but their thoughts were running in a stream far above mine. I felt tired then but I did not rest easy.

Later, I was not the only one watching as Charlie turned the rock carefully in his hands. It was a small, dull-looking thing. He pushed my branches to one side so that the morning sun fell on it, and then the patterns showed: red veins branched across it; at the end of one branch were dark swirls, at the end of the other, a shine. The shine was not visible in the shade, only in the sunlight did this spot shine like a mirror.

'Wow,' said Charlie quietly to himself. The rock felt warm and heavy in his cupped hands, then I felt all his being lift; the very brain in his head was rising. Everything about him strained upwards, then gradually he settled back into himself.

'This is it, Ash. Phase two is here. Adapt and survive. That's what the garden has to do, and there's no time to waste, no time at all.' He swung one-armed down the rope.

Just then Eva came out cradling some bugs she'd rescued from a cabbage. She was about to free them when she stumbled and almost fell into the mini crater.

'What the…?' she said looking down, up and all around. 'Have we been bombed?'

'Meteor,' said Charlie. 'Seen my library card? Got to go,' and he skidded through the house.

A few nights later the excitement was over apart from the hole in the garden, and a few moles still shocked by the sudden air in their tunnels. Eva wanted to take the rock to the museum but Charlie worried that he wouldn't get it back, so he kept it in the treehouse and did tests on it. He found that it did funny things to magnets. Sometimes he just stared at it like his mind could follow it back out to where it came from.

Wilfred came to see me. I hadn't seen him for a while. He'd been in the hills two counties away, he said, at a meeting. He inspected the hole and shook his head.

'Strange days, one more omen.'

'Of what?' I asked.

Wilfred peered into the hole and shuddered. He raised himself onto his hind legs and sniffed the wind: 'It's coming soon, I see it.'

'Can't anybody give a straight answer round here?'

'We must wait for the council. Mother Pica will dwell on the signs we have gathered; when she is ready she will speak.'

He asked me lots of questions about the rock.

'Branches—choices most likely. The shine—the future I would guess *if* we make the right choice.'

'Or maybe it's just another rock,' I said.

'Or maybe it's just another rock. Don't balance on the fence too long, my friend. You may get blown off.'

16

Science

I watched with interest as what looked like a giant woolly caterpillar walked up the garden. What an odd creature, I thought. Only when it came into my shade and looked up did I know it for Wilfred. He had grown his coat, so that his eyes were set deep in fur, which haloed his body, doubling his size.

'Wilfred,' I greeted him, 'expecting a cold snap?'

'I start North tomorrow. My area runs from Greenland to the Barents, then South to Germany. I'm collecting proxy votes from those who can't travel, then I head into the Black Forest for the great gathering. I need your decision before I go. Are you with us? Can I tell the gathering that there may be a way to get the plants on board?'

'Exactly what do you want me to do?'

'I want you to teach the plants to think so we can all join forces against the humans.'

'Against—what do you mean against?'

'That's the point of the vote.

'First ballot: is the planet better off without humans?

'Ballot 2: If it is, what action should we take? Non-cooperation—cows don't give milk, hens don't lay and so on, like the practice run we had a few months back, or b) aggression, like the hamster rebellion.'

'I need more time to think.'

'There is no time; I start tonight.'

There was a soft sliding sound followed by thuds as a pile of books slid down the chute. Then came a pillow; then came Charlie.

This was a relief. Wilfred wouldn't hang around with Charlie there.

'I'll be back later for your answer, and don't forget, you owe me one,' Wilfred hissed.

'Hi Ash.' Charlie came elbowing out of the chute, sat down and started to read.

'What's this?' I asked.

'Phase two,' he said without looking up.

Now usually I like to look over Charlie's shoulder as he reads his science books. They are fun, colourful things with optical illusions and pop-up models of volcanoes and spacecraft. Not these new books: these books had page after page of tiny writing, and chemical equations and weird diagrams. Charlie read following his finger at great speed, line after line; the pages turned almost as fast as a breeze could blow them. When I tried speaking to him he answered, 'Just a minute,' but as he got deeper into the books he didn't answer at all. He wasn't being rude, he just couldn't hear. I looked into his mind and it was full of words and symbols running by in endless strings. Every now and then he'd pause for a few seconds and the strings would rearrange themselves and link up with other strings in different patterns, then he'd whisper, 'Okay, got it,' and go racing on again. He finished a whole fat book without looking up once. Between books he rolled the space rock around in his hands.

Since catching the falling star, Charlie was a boy possessed. Phase two was much more than a schoolboy project. As far as I could tell his aim was to read every science book in the world. First he hauled as much as he could carry from the library, then he asked Conal's dad, who's a nurse, to get some books from the hospital library.

Normally I hung around listlessly while he read, wishing that we could have fun together like we used to, but that night I had some deep thinking of my own to do. I knew that Wilfred would be back soon demanding my decision. Knowing all about Wilfred and his powers of persuasion, I guessed that the first vote would go against the humans.

I looked down fondly at the top of Charlie's head, where his hair grew in a funny swirl. He was in a growth spurt, lengthening out and losing roundness.

'Now then, did someone put manure in your wellies?' I muttered—that's what Les Durrell said to his growing nephew. It was my favourite-ever line from *Brooke Farm* and I'd been waiting for a chance to say it. But it was wasted: Charlie was still too engrossed to notice me.

Was I wrong to speak up for humans just because of Charlie? Wouldn't he end up like the rest of them in a few years time? He broke from his reading as though he sensed my thoughts and gave me a reassuring look. I looked at the dancing speckles in his eyes, eyes that had never lost the astonishment of being born, and knew that I would stick by him all his life or mine.

So who would put the case for the humans at the great gathering? No one I guessed.

Eva wandered out into the garden. It looked like she had her painting itch.

'Are you all right, sweetheart?' she called to Charlie as she carted out her easel, paints and stool and set up at the top of the orchard.

'Yes,' Charlie called back without looking up.

Eva painted. I looked at the garden, much of it still drab in its winter starkness, then I looked at her painting. She had the trees in a layered net against the white sky; soft greens and duns and yellows underneath; finally she dabbed on white flames of magnolia and balls of apple blossom, whiter than the sky. She was so intent, so lifted, and her aura showed a special strength of light pouring out of her forehead. And then I got it. I knew why she painted.

'I get it. I get beauty,' I said to Charlie, but he didn't hear. 'I get beauty,' I told Holly, but she wasn't listening. Glorious, glorious, I thought; and surely, this alone is worth saving the humans for.

When Eva finished painting, and Charlie, too, came up for air, it was dusk.

'Bye, Ash,' he said and climbed back up the chute.

'Hi and bye—is that it? Is that all I get nowadays?'

I didn't mean Charlie to hear this but he came back to the window and spoke in a muffled voice: 'Don't sulk, you know how important this is.'

I did know, and he shamed me. The garden didn't end at the fence, it went on and on, and he wanted to save it all. Eva and her art, Charlie and his projects. Was it imagination, the feeling of a deep, deliberate scoring into my trunk? This is what I felt on the human side: IIIIIIIII, on the vermin side, this: IIIIIIII. I knew what I had to do.

Charlie put on his pyjamas, lit a candle and opened yet another book. When it was fully dark Eva came to check on him.

'Time you were asleep,' she said; 'shall I take the book?'

'Just a minute, just a minute,' he said, holding one hand up; 'ah now I get it,' and he scribbled a few notes. 'Okay, I'm ready,' and he flopped back on his pillows, a boy again.

Eva looked at the book.

'You're really reading this?'

'Mmm, it's all right for background, but I really need net access for the latest research.'

'On postgraduate genetic engineering?'

'Mum, it's important.'

There are times, I'm learning, when odd things happen and somehow it's best not to ask questions but just to go with the flow. Eva seemed to have one of those moments of faith.

'I'll see what I can do,' she said, and blew softly on the candle.

That was enough of a signal for Wilfred. I swear he'd been waiting under the hedge all that time, sweating in his big woolly coat. He bustled out.

'Well, have you decided?'

'I've decided.'

He looked surprised. 'What's it to be then?'

'I'll do my best to spread gnosis in the plant world. I'm willing to teach them how, but not what to think.'

'Good, Ash, others can...'

'Wait. There's one condition. My guess is that no one will speak for the humans at the first motion. I want you to put my point of view by proxy, please.'

Wilfred listened and spluttered, 'You know, you owe me. I wasn't expecting conditions.'

'I didn't want to bring this up, but Charlie ended up saving you.'

'That's rubbish. I was just baiting Adolf. I would've made it.'

Underneath the swagger I heard it. Self-doubt. I had him, if I could just stand firm. Roots help in these circumstances. Legs make for haste and impatience I've found. Time was running out for Wilfred, while I was going nowhere, so at last he agreed.

As I watched him dash away like a big furry hedgehog, I had a smug feeling that I'd got the best of the meeting.

With Wilfred gone and Charlie still possessed by his reading marathon, I was left to my own devices. I contemplated the weather, I watched the birds, the bees and the ever-changing sky, but I needed more. I needed human contact. I was, you could say, addicted.

Graham was out for much of the day so I sprouted more branches and found that I could look into the flat above, which belonged to Bob. Bob was retired and watched a lot of TV. He liked the history channel. I'm sure he never realised that the little twig, tapping at his window as he watched, was his companion. One day we were watching a programme about the Stone Age. Bob wasn't paying much attention; he prefers war programmes. I, on the other hand, was most interested to see what these stone-agers were like, since Wilfred had approved of them. 'The Stone Age,' said the man on the screen, 'spanned the period from 10,000—2000BC.'

I was so startled that I whipped the window with my branches and Bob looked up from stirring his tea. 'Impossible,' I said to the man on the screen, who rudely carried on talking, 'Wilfred can't be more than two thousand years old.'

I started reckoning: if I had been alive for all that time I would be very fat indeed with two thousand rings in my trunk; I would be twice as big as the grand old yew in the churchyard, which needs iron bands to hold up its branches. 'Your berries give long life,' I remembered Charlie saying when he was researching Rowan legends. Hmm, Wilfred was quite greedy and possessive with my berries.

Oh, he was a wily one. And I'd been congratulating

myself for getting the better of him; he must have seen straight through me. I worried that he would find a tricky way round my decision.

After a few weeks, Charlie ran out of reading material. Graham let Charlie use his laptop for research, and when he got stuck he e-mailed a man called Will Yates. He is the first human to have a chip put in his brain (wood or potato I'm not sure), and for some reason this makes him very, very clever. People from all over the world ask him questions, but they don't like his answers, so they say something is wrong with his chip. Charlie was very excited when Will Yates e-mailed back, and they kept up a little correspondence. Charlie also made wire models of cages and spirals with knobs on. He fiddled with these endlessly, talking to himself and to me as he worked.

'Why are *you* doing this?' I wanted to know.

'It's my job,' said Charlie.

'But, you're only eleven; if you want a job you should get a paper round. And why is it all so urgent?'

'Things are changing very fast, too fast for life to keep up. It's all here in the rock,' he spun the space rock in the vault of my branches, but to me it still looked unremarkable. 'It's up to science to fast track evolution. It's our only hope, Ash. So—that's my job.'

17

The Vote

It was blossom day; not for me; my peak is some weeks later, but for the cherries. Eva says this is her favourite day of the year because on blossom day all summer lies ahead. The cherry blossom is maxed out: full, heavy, dropping with blossom; and the trees are holding, holding their heavenliness. The ground plants are outclassed, as they are in autumn; everyone is looking upwards at blossom on blue. After that peak of loveliness the snowing starts. Petals drift down with a wedding feeling.

Up the dappled spring garden Wilfred walked, but how slowly, how unlike himself. Ponderous of paw he was, a gravity about him. Half a year since I'd seen him, yet I wished that Wilfred had not come because suddenly I feared for the day. My rustling leaves drooped quietly as Wilfred came into my shade. We dispensed with our usual greetings.

'It's all done then,' I said.

‘Signed and sealed,’ said Wilfred. I tried to read in his eyes which way the vote had gone but I couldn’t. I sighed and thought of all the people I’d got to know on Overvale Road.

Few of them knew of me but I still thought of them as friends. We were all in it together you see. I had an urge sometimes to stretch my branches out and shelter them all. None of them had any idea how their fate balanced on a stem just then. I wanted to put off knowing, to let them keep their world a little longer.

‘Begin at the beginning,’ I said to Wilfred, ‘start with the journey, you know how I like a tale.’

So he began his story in the glorious spring garden, though with more listeners than he knew.

‘I travelled courtesy of man to begin with; by train and ferry and fishing boat. I’m well practised and pride myself that I can get anywhere in the planet within a week or two. Only once did I feel afraid and that was on the last lap. Gruichin Beach was my destination: as remote as you can imagine. For the last fifty miles I had to hitch a ride with a hawk. I have ridden with a hawk before, but that first time I was no volunteer, and as I felt the horrid, familiar grip, all the terror of it came back to me.

‘I was a youngster again. The feel of the hawk’s grip, so firm; my frail ribs pinned by the bony talons; my breath stopped; the good earth with all its hidey holes and cover, dropping away. So exposed, nothing but air below, feathers and talons above, nowhere to hide but the barred breast of my murderer. It dropped me, useless, on a rocky ledge. I looked into its yellow saucer eyes. Its greedy chicks like great downy boulders waited. One foot held me down and its beak descended for the first tear, then it turned its awful profile away and leapt flapping at a human child who was climbing down the cliffs hunting for eggs. It was the only time I've had cause to be grateful to a human. I went over the ledge, scrabbled vertically for some way, then fell, as the cliff receded, into some bushes.

'That adventure had been no more than a pinprick of a distant memory, but it swelled and filled my mind like yesterday as we flew, and all the time I wondered if my carrier might not think better of the proceedings and veer off to some ledge where her hungry chicks awaited. But at last she dropped me at Gruichin Beach, and I stumbled on shaking legs to the gathering. I was late. In the blue-black ocean, fins of all sizes broke the surface with flashes of grey and silver and blue. A whale spouted in the bay; seabirds and seals massed on the rocks.

'I was escorted to an outcrop, which hung over the ocean and from there I put the questions to the gathering. Penguins swam around the bay and bustled among the rocks collecting votes. At last all the votes were in and the reps filed or swooped past me with the results. Things were going well; every vote was against man, and I was pleased with the good sense being shown by these truly wild animals; then a very large penguin stepped up carrying the vote of the dolphins. The dolphins, as I told you before, are the only animals, apart from man, where the entire species has gnosis, so their block vote is very large.

' "What say the dolphins?" ' I asked.

' "The dolphins vote for man," said the penguin. They also send you this message: "Wilfred, in your heart you will be asking why we have voted this way. The humans want to be our friends but as yet they have not learned wisdom. Their own terrible mistakes are now so great that wisdom will be forced upon them. Even now they are turning and twisting away from it, but nature has them by the scruff and will open their eyes. We must give them a chance to learn that lesson."

Wilfred sighed and shook his head. 'The council once asked the dolphins to take leadership of the animal kingdom but they refused. Power does not attract them. They are generous creatures, and I'm afraid, quite blind to evil. But they are entitled to their views, so I recited the messenger's oath:

' "I promise that all votes entrusted to me, be they yea or nay, shall be faithfully delivered to council."

'I left my tail print in the mud where it will not be disturbed until it becomes a fossil and I turned away from the dolphins playing so joyously as the sea turned milky in the sunset.

'Their backing for man was a blow, but the balance swung back my way as I journeyed South towards the Black Forest, collecting votes as I went. As I made my final run, following a stream that ran down into the forest, I was already imagining a world without vermin.

My hopes were high as I trotted into camp, but they soared far higher when I saw what lay before me.

'The gathering was greater and more impressive than I had imagined. Creatures were there from every continent: bright-plumed exotics, swivel-eyed lizards, stripes, spots and scales; and the more I looked the more I saw; leaves became insects, logs stood up and walked; all the secret clearing seethed with life. What intrepid and ingenious travellers these animals were. Sighted miles from their own lands, they were presumed to have escaped from zoos. Zoos, bah!' he spat in disgust. 'Others left only fearsome signs: giant paw prints in farmyards—the seeds of legends, if there is time enough left now for legend-making.

'I was proud as I looked at them: this, I hoped, was the future; these would be the mothers and fathers of a new order, the Kingdom of animals, creatures with the knowing of humans but without their worst flaws: greed, vanity and cruelty. That was my dream.

'There were lots of fringe meetings that night and, as I ran around eavesdropping, I grew more and more encouraged.

'With the first light of day we were all up and busy. The Pica took up her position in the clearing, perched on a tree that had fallen across two others, forming a kind of bridge. Her first task was to receive the signs.

'The animals came forward and laid their signs at her feet for the reading: a branch from Belize, a root from Siberia; some simply bore witness. Then we waited. The Pica studied the signs and listened to the tales for twelve days. At last she spoke: of the fate of the planet, of the fauna and flora, and of the humans.

'Ash, we escape the worst—for now, and so do they. They must be the luckiest creatures in creation. The oil wars have saved them from the scorching, the fiery waters and the final flood.'

'But I thought war was a bad thing.'

'And so it is, a terrible thing, but you see, without oil they cannot wreck the earth so quickly, so we are all saved from the worst end. But there is still great change to come, great heat and floods. Much life will suffer and die.

'The Pica called the animals back in turn so that she could tell them where to go in order to survive the changes. A few were given wide lands, some must seek out tiny regions where they will still struggle. When it was my turn I was told that I could remain here, but I would need all my wits to survive, or I could move higher and more northerly and have an easier time of it. I believe I will stay. I always did like a challenge. After me the gopi hopped up, a cousin of mine, so shy they are not even known to man. The Pica's sharp eyes turned soft: "I am sorry," she said, "there is nowhere for you to go."

' "Nowhere," said the gopi, "in all the planet, no place for us?"

' "I am sorry," said the Pica again.

'The gopi turned and walked sadly away. She was not alone. Many others started their walk, saw the Pica shaking her head in sorrow, and turned away.

'One in fifty, Ash; only one in fifty species will survive the changes. She expects the plants to suffer equal losses.'

Just then a noise I'd never heard before came from behind the coop, something between a sneeze and a hiccup.

'Come out,' said Wilfred, 'you're safe here.'

Another strange noise, a snuffly squeak.

In the shadows behind the coop I could see a sort of rat bunny with round amber eyes; it was twice the size of Wilfred.

'It's my cousin, the gopi. She's too shy to come out. I brought her home to try her luck with me. If we go down, we go down together.'

Another shy hiccup.

'This is the Teacher tree I have spoken of.'

Two golden saucer eyes gleamed up at me.

'Anyway,' Wilfred went on, 'the Pica began the list of those not present who would also be lost from the earth forever: the majestic polar bear, exquisite rain forest butterflies, and on and on. Fish and fowl will soon spawn and soar for the last time. Flowers will open to the sun for the last time. Then I was angry. I tore around the forest, throwing up earth, shredding leaves and branches. I do believe if I had met a man then, I would have killed him, small as I am. I returned to the gathering. All around me there was anger and sorrow as we prepared to vote. I had no doubts at all then which way it would go.

'The Pica read the motion.

' "Who speaks against man?" she said. It took a long

time for so many to file past. I hailed my friend the parrot from Senegal; he repaid me in full with his scathing speech. My speech against was probably the longest and received the most rousing cheer.

' "Now, who speaks for?" the Pica said.

'A ruffled sparrow flew into the clearing and perched on the log.

' "Sparrow, England. I speak for the humans. They feed us in winter."

'Weak, I thought. "Who took your food in the first place?" I muttered.

'A cat strolled into the circle. She licked her lips at the sparrow, who fluttered nervously away; then she spoke unhurriedly.

' "Cat, France. I speak for. No other species but man is foolish enough to feed and house another for no return. We cats have learned to use that foolishness to our advantage; others could do the same."

'Next up was a dog.

' "Dog, Germany. I speak for. Humans make good leaders. They provide well for their pack."

'Laughable. Then there was silence.

' "Are there any other speakers?"

'I walked into the circle. Rustles, flutters and all manner of animal sounds ran around the gathering.

' "I am charged with delivering a proxy speech for Tree, England."

'At this, another flurry of surprise and questioning looks.

' "Tree sends these words:

> I speak for. What do humans bring to the world? Without them who would swoon at sunsets? Who would make art and music? Who would seek beyond appearances? Who would question? Who would laugh?

'The words were choking me but I pressed on.

> Human science is born of questions, and science might yet save us all. Man has found a way to help life adapt and survive the changes ahead. Through science there is hope for all.

'You might like to know that there was a storm of reaction to your speech. I walked round the circle listening.

' "What are these things: art, laughter, music?" I heard them ask. "And what does the sunset gain from being swooned at?" But louder than this I heard voices lifted in hope: "man is clever; man will help us survive."

'Of course I tried to put them right on this, but the damage was done.

' "You have had many months to consider the issues," the Pica said, "my advice would be: do not consider what you do not understand. Look around you, use the evidence of your own senses, and vote."

'And they voted. The cats, dogs and sparrows, backed by the large dolphin vote were joined by many threatened species in the for camp; such is the power of hope. The two camps looked to be split evenly. The younger Pica counted and recounted before finally declaring a hung vote. The casting vote went to the great Pica.

‘ “Ah what a burden,” she said, lowering her black-hooded head. Minutes passed before she raised it and spoke.

‘ “For,” she declared, and I felt winded with disappointment. My supporters were with me, I could read in their faces the sigh for what might have been.

‘ “With conditions,” the Pica went on. “You may have heard rumours that gnosis has arisen among the flora, and indeed Wilfred has given a statement on their behalf. This puts us in a very powerful position. The humans can survive without other animals, but not without plants; on the other hand, it may be that we all need human science to survive the changes ahead.

‘ “I propose that we support the humans on condition that they vow to respect this planet, to live without hierarchy, and strive to preserve the balance of nature.

‘ “They should know that we can withdraw our support at any time. We can make these demands now because we have a bridge to human consciousness, tree to boy. I have had the boy watched for some time now. He will lead. He will speak for them all.”

‘Groups of my supporters had gathered and I heard their mutterings. It’s not over yet, there will be more demonstrations and uprisings, but how much better if we had all united against them.

‘I didn’t hang around, I hopped on a log and drifted through the forest for days. Sun, shade, moonlight, passed over me again and again but I had no will to move. I had a vision of that river running on to the end of the world, of myself on the log tipping over the edge, plunging.

'Men brought me back, men with their meddling. The usual reaction to a dead rat on a log is indifference, unless you intend to eat it. Hundreds of animals must have seen me on my journey through the forest. All left me alone. Only man has to have a poke. So I found myself being poked. I dived and swam, leaving three boys splashing around behind me.

'With the cold water and the hunger I felt a sudden clarity. The Pica voted wisely. We don't need to do anything. Science got mankind into this mess, I don't believe it will get them out of it. The weather itself will shoot them down.'

I looked around me again and it seemed that the sky was too blue, the blossom too pure, touched with sadness, like all beauty, because it cannot last.

18

Fire and Drought

It was Graham's birthday. The humans were enjoying a dry spell which had stretched from March well into June. I was not. My roots were locked in baked soil: imagine walking twenty miles on a hot day without a drink, while wearing wooden clogs a size too small, and you might have some idea how draught feels to a plant. The gardeners weren't allowed to use hosepipes. Eva did what she could with the watering can; but our root hairs were only teased by the little damp that reached them. We longed for rain.

It seemed a long while back when Charlie first explained to me about human dreams. I didn't understand at the time but now I think I do. Dreams can show you your deepest longings. I had my first dream: I dreamed of a thundery smell; fat summer drops breaking on my leaves and darkening the soil; then that first surge of living water through my empty vessels, sucked in one glorious pull through to my leaves which filled out and rebounded glossily in the still hammering rain. Then I woke and it was back to the tight clogs.

Anyway, as I said, it was Graham's birthday and to celebrate he was having a barbecue. All the neighbours were there. The neighbours had grown very close since the oil wars: they helped each other with their various skills, there was Marion, the sewing lady; John, the carpenter; several gardeners—their skills were in great demand; Graham, the mechanic; and they all shared and walked and talked like they never used to in their car days. I looked over into Graham's garden and it was lively and noisy, with neighbours swapping tips on ingenious ways to save power and grow your own food, and get solar panels put in on the cheap. There was a smell of smoke and roast meat, and they drank Graham's home brew, which was very strong, and Marion's damson wine, which was also very strong, and soon there was as much laughter as there was conversation.

When it grew dusk, Graham lit a bonfire and everyone sat around on the yellow grass, all very happy, listening to the fire crackling and settling in the night air. Charlie and Conal sat together on a log, their eyes lit by fire. Eva and Brigid slipped away for a few minutes, then they came to the French doors and called everyone in. The doors were wide open and I could see and hear inside. Eva had made a cake for Graham, covered in real melted chocolate. Chocolate, by then, was an expensive treat. Graham blew out his candles and made a speech:

'I've lived in this road for nine years and till last year

I didn't know any of you. You probably thought of me as that nuisance who rides motorbikes up and down the street at all hours of day and night. All I knew of you was which car was parked outside which house. It's only recently, since we've all had to pull together, that I've really got to know my neighbours, so…hello.' Then he giggled a bit as he was quite drunk. 'I do miss my bikes—I do. What I'm trying to say is we've all lost something, but what we've found is,' he raised his glass and looked directly at Eva, 'better.'

Eva raised her glass to him.

Charlie looked at them both thoughtfully.

'Hear, hear,' everyone chorused. Then they ate.

'Mmm, so long since I've had chocolate.'

'Oh, this is so good.'

Then silence with a few groans of pleasure.

Thankfully, manure, unlike cocoa, does not have to be imported, only carted from the nearest pigsty. However, I would have given up manure for a year just then for one good draught of water.

My attention drifted down Graham's garden. It was all pale and dry as straw. If only the wind would change and bring that rain down from the North. There was a gust as if in answer to my wish. Burning paper lifted from the edge of the bonfire and dropped down at the edge of the compost heap. The baby flames grew instantly strong, as though a fire dimension impatiently lapped through into our own. Within seconds rabid flames ran along to some bin bags. I watched as a plastic bag shrivelled from the rubbish inside like disintegrating skin from a skeleton. Something in the bag caught fiercely: Graham's oil-soaked rags or overalls I think. The strengthening breeze lifted one blazing flag over the fence and out of sight.

I called to Charlie, 'Look up, look up,' but he, like the others, was too transported by the chocolate to listen. Eventually, Bob looked up and noticed the fire running wickedly towards Graham's shed. Everyone spilled into the garden.

'Get water,' someone called.

'There's buckets in the shed,' Graham shouted. Flames swarmed around the shed even as he ran towards it.

'Where's your hosepipe? No don't tell me, it's in the shed.'

'There is no water,' Graham remembered. 'It's off till tomorrow morning.'

'Better get the fire brigade,' said Eva.

The hedge behind the shed was alight too. Now that was painful to watch; the outside was dry and shrivelled but I knew its heart was green and burning.

Just then all of us—Charlie, Eva, the whole garden, me— were swallowed, enfolded in a noise; a swollen, bass, ba-room.

In the pause it flashed through my mind that Wilfred's end of days had come. I waited for the sky to fall.

'What was that?' Brigid said.

'It's bomb testing at Barrow,' said Conal.

But the black smoke mushroom did not hang over

Barrow Point; it rose from just beyond the fence and blew over Fortress Sperrin.

Graham swore under his breath, ran up to the attic and poked his head through the skylight.

'Whoa,' he exhaled from somewhere above me.

'What is it?' Eva called up.

'Sperrin's annexe, it's burning like crazy.'

Charlie joined him and they shouted a commentary down to the rest of the neighbours. They saw the fire engines stuck in the old town's narrow lanes finally coming out at Stoop Top and then, their sirens screaming over Graham's voice, lights pulsing through the trees, they swung up on both sides, one outside Sperrin's and one in front of Graham's house. Eva and Charlie went up to our own attic to watch.

At Sperrin's a line of neighbours gathered in a row, arms folded, speculating; their eyes and faces lit with heat as great cables of water battered the fire, while another vehicle came leisurely up Stoop Lane. One of the very few cars out after dark, it was a black four-wheel drive and it carried the Sperrins homewards. Charlie got out his telescope for this, Sperrin's arrival.

'He looks like he's going to burst something,' said Charlie, 'the firemen are holding him back. Fire's jumping down his line of soldiers, all their heads blazing—weird. He's struggling—looks like he's fighting with one of the firemen. Wind's blowing flames towards his house—he's got away, running for the gate. Another fireman's got him now, two of them, leading him away. There's Oona; she's cool.'

On Graham's side the last frill of sparks was battered into wet blackness. The hedge was saved but the shed was just a few black stumps with bicycle frames standing up in between. Sperrin's fire was fiercer. Fuelled from within, the flames shrunk down under the water, shook themselves and jumped back to double height.

What had made the garage explode like that, everyone wanted to know. Charlie and Eva knew.

Charlie carried on with his commentary: 'Mr Jack from over the road is talking to Sperrin. Now he's running back towards his car, but the fire engine is blocking him in. He's ranting and raving about something. Another fire engine's coming. Flames are smaller now. It's all deadening down; the tunnel's gone and there's not much left of the garage—looks like a blast hole in the roof.'

One other unexpected bonus: all of Graham's garden got a very thorough soaking with water, and my roots push quite a way under the hedge on that side. I took a long, steady and very welcome drink.

Eventually the firemen were satisfied that the scene was safe and the neighbours drifted back into their houses except for Mr Jack who had a long conversation with Sperrin. Charlie saw him pointing back to his own house and then gesturing up towards us. Sperrin got into his car. Charlie came down to the treehouse.

'I've got witnesses.' Sperrin burst past Graham into his garden. 'A-hah, I can see for myself. What sort of idiot builds a bonfire on a day like this? Mrs Jack saw it from her sickbed. Fire coming over your fence and landing in my hedge clippings. I expect compensation from you; do you know how much…?' he checked himself.

'I'm sure your insurance will cover it,' Graham tried.

'This is criminal negligence. You'll be hearing from my lawyer.'

Charlie coughed and Sperrin looked up. Eva and Charlie were leaning forward, watching eagerly from my branches. Eva broke into giggles. Charlie's laugh streamed out under hers, and then Graham too cracked. The three of them were more and more gripped by their sense of humour, it split their faces, it made their bodies jerk and buckle. Sperrin's odd fish-mouth hung open in his smoke-dirty face.

'Mrs Slater and brat! Misfortune's a joke to you, is it?' He turned to Graham. 'Did she put you up to this? Taken in by a pretty face, were you? I'll see the lot of you in court.'

He turned and tripped over a hosepipe. Laughter followed him down the alley.

Something clicked inside me. It was connected to that moment when Sperrin looked up into two faces, two people stuck up a tree. I felt a swirling in the fattest part of my trunk and I wanted to do that ha-ha thing. Excitement came over me like a delicious warm shower. What a great feeling. I was getting a sense of humour.

19

Of Floods and Heroes

Wilfred could be wrong but all the signs and my own instincts said he was right. Each day brought new reports of droughts and flooding and ever bigger weather.

The heat of that summer was like none I'd ever known. The previous year was a minor rehearsal. Brassclash, Charlie and I named it. Even the humans stopped glorying in the sun—like fools welcoming the executioner, Wilfred said—and started to ask, how much hotter can it get, and when will it end? Night brought no relief. Brigid brought the cart round after sunset so that they could all ride with a breeze on their faces. It was too hot to sleep so at midnight they waded in the sea.

There were many deaths in the gardens and among the people. The Jungle had never looked so brown and withered. The strong green aura, which shimmered above it, was pale and yellowing. Our greatest loss was Beech. Seventy summers she had seen, but this was one hot summer too many. She died. Water was strictly rationed. Eva could not help us. What moisture I could get I conserved at my centre. There was no choice but to let my outer branches die. I passed through the tight clogs stage. I could no longer feel my roots at all.

I realised how sick I was when I couldn't follow the plot of *Brooke Farm*. Charlie was very worried; he mulched around my roots and talked about building a canopy over me if the weather did not break soon. Seeing that events were speeding up, he turned to his science books in a new fury of reading. I might have given up but I sensed relief was coming, if I could just hold out a week or two longer.

Charlie looked around the clear blue sky. 'Feel anything, Ash? Can you feel cloud anywhere in this half of the planet?'

I showed him what I sensed.

'There's chains and curtains of diamonds being hoovered off the sea. All that water funnelling up. It's a long way off though. And will it come this way?' he wondered.

I didn't know.

At last dawn broke behind clouds. The sky darkened and darkened, till at midday it was as black as I had ever seen it.

Then it came. Splat: one, two, three, a hundred, a thousand thousand drops of splattering, rattling, hammering, rain. Underneath was hush; the rain hush, a sort of pause and shock. The plants receive, the birds are stilled and quieted, humans stop and shelter.

At first I gloried; the water surging through my cracked vessels was almost painful. I drank and drank until every cell of every leaf was full to bursting. The way it rained was as though a century's water was stored up in the sky, and then some god tipped it all out in one day. The rain came and came and came again. I stood in woozy abandon, aware of nothing but the rain. Then Charlie came out and stood laughing beside me, the rain thumping onto his upturned face.

The dusty earth took it all for a day and night before it started to pool around my roots. In the morning the rain eased and everything steamed in the sun. It was Charlie's last day at school. Eva let him cycle down Spring Hill since it was almost free of traffic. Where once it had been jammed with cars it had become sweet with tree breath from the woods at the top. In the morning it was a-sing with birds and bicycle bells and careering children arriving at school in a breath-taking free-wheeling rush; others dawdled through puddles, stopping to feed grass to the sheep or pick wet-faced flowers from the grateful verges.

At midday I scented rain again, then came a vision that unnerved me. The tea cup, with the deep blue tea, frothed violently and started an endless overflow. Uneasily my mind searched for Charlie. There he was, sitting in his classroom under a summer collage of cotton-wool clouds, chewing his pencil.

Even as I looked at him, the classroom darkened and a great crack of thunder ripped the sky. Sheet rain slid over the windows; then came a train of flicker and boom, and after each boom, the rain seemed to press heavier. Beyond the thunder I thought I heard something scarier: a terrible, breaking rush.

Charlie looked up from chewing his pencil to see a stream creeping across the floor. His first thought was that someone had peed themselves; then he looked to the art sink to see if it had overflowed. Other children were looking too. Then, 'Miss, Miss, look!' The teacher's heels clattered through the wet; she opened the door and the water came in.

Eva came out, catching my attention. She held a coat tented above her head. Looking over the hedge, she caught her breath at the water thundering down Spring Hill. The morning's muddy stream had become a brown torrent. She stood frozen, water running into her nose and mouth.

'Charlie,' she whispered.

She grabbed to the phone and jabbed at three or four different numbers.

'Where are they all?' she shouted and threw the phone down.

The thunder cracked again; the rain came with a new crushing weight. Eva ran from the house. My roots had loosened in the soft ground. I actually leaned over a fraction with my great desire to run after her. All my branches were alive, probing. There was something about the weather that I had never felt before, not even in the great storm of '87. What was it? It felt unbounded; it felt as though anything could happen. 'The weather itself will shoot them down,' Wilfred had said. I could only feel that he was right. All my life I had looked on the weather as a mother; now it felt like an outlaw.

Minutes later I heard an oddly thrilling, growling roar; a sound which tore the air. It was familiar but I couldn't quite place it. Soon after, I thought I heard clopping from the street, not the steady rhythm I knew, but an urgent pounding.

Over and over I tried to reach Charlie but all I got was interference and tree thoughts. 'Be careful what you wish for,' Sally Durrell had said to Les. I wished that I hadn't wished quite so hard for rain. There was nothing to do but watch as water filled up the world. Around me every hollow became a puddle, every dip a pond. I saw Hilda peer out of the coop, which stood like a river hut on stilts in the pooling water. The wooden steps through the Jungle had become a waterfall. The rushing came again, louder, swifter more terrible, and then the sirens started.

I lost all feeling of time, letting myself drown in my old green state as my fears grew. At last I heard sounds. Brigid and Conal came down the alleyway, found the spare key in the greenhouse and let themselves into the kitchen. Brigid looked around worriedly, rubbed a towel through her hair, then sat down at the kitchen table to wait. After a while she went to the sitting room and got a fire going. She found the old clothes horse and hung towels and blankets in front of the fire to warm.

'I need windscreen wipers for my eyes.' Charlie's voice snapped me back to life. He was somewhere very near.

I could see him, one eye closed with water streaming out of his hair, the other blinking into the rain.

Soon, the kitchen door opened and in trailed Eva and Charlie, their clothes hanging from them with the weight of water. Charlie was laughing and all my fear fell away. They stripped off, wrapped up in warm blankets, and raised hot drinks with still shaking hands. At first it was difficult to understand what Eva said through her chattering teeth, but this is what she told Brigid:

'I ran out into the street. I was going to take a pool car, but they were gone. The emergency car had gone too. I started running towards Stoop Lane, then Graham, bless him, pulled up on a motor bike.'

'Not just any bike,' Charlie interrupted, 'a Harley V-pod; you should see it.'

'I wouldn't have cared if it was a penny farthing so long as it had a motor.'

The metal monster did have its uses then.

'Anyway,' Eva continued, 'he whizzed me down the hill but we couldn't get further than the church. That's when we saw Conal in a crocodile of kids being led uphill. He told me that Charlie was washed away in the second rush of water. I was nearly hysterical. George's dad had binoculars. He said that there were children on the school roof and one child stranded in a tree. Straightaway I thought, 'That's Charlie.' He let me look and it was.'

I sent my thanks to the tree.

Eva went on: 'We were opposite that row of boarded-up shops and a chap from the old water sports shop came over. He said he had a couple of dinghies, would they be any use? Graham got in a dinghy and paddled out to the tree. The water was still rising and pushing us further back. I watched through the binoculars. I could see Charlie's tree but I couldn't see Charlie any more. Graham was leaning out of the dinghy trying to grab the tree trunk. He lunged at it, the dinghy slid away from him and he disappeared under the water, but he bobbed up, scrambled back into the boat and tried again. Then I saw Charlie's legs dangling below the leaves. There was a current running past the tree and Graham was paddling to stay in one place. Charlie was swinging from a branch…'

'And Graham was shouting to me,' Charlie interrupted; 'he said don't let go till I say. He got the dinghy steady, then he shouted "now" and spread his arms out to catch me, but when he stopped paddling the boat started drifting, and I had to swing myself out and then I dropped on top of him.'

Charlie giggled while Eva went on:

'There was this tangle of arms and legs and the boat tipped right up on its edge but they hung on and Graham started paddling back.'

'And the dinghy was going down fast; I think I burst it when I dropped into it.'

'I rushed into the water and nearly drowned trying to pull the boat in.'

'Then Graham got us clear on the Harley. He's gone back to help the others.'

‘I hope he’s okay,’ Eva said, and her eyes were soft.

We came up Stoop Lane, and guess who was out in his driveway shouting into his phone? ‘If a drop of that flood water reaches me, heads will roll.’

‘Was Sperrin complaining to God?’ Charlie asked.

It was dark before we heard the roar of Graham’s Harley. Eva ran out and brought him in. What a sight. Charlie handed him an old shirt of Pete’s and he settled down with a quilt round his shoulders to tell the rest of the story. He saw the children air-lifted from the roof of the school. He managed to rescue a girl from a telegraph pole and an old woman who was trying to hold on to a drainpipe while gripping a budgie cage. Eventually they all sat quietly thoughtful in front of the dying fire.

‘And you know why it happened?’ said Wilfred, in the blessed cool of the next morning. ‘The seas of the world were all high and swollen with the heat and the ice melt. A broken river had gone to meet a swollen sea. The animals haven’t suffered too much, we saw it coming and headed for high ground but I couldn’t resist going back to watch the chaos and the breakdown.’

He must have felt my disapproval.

‘Why not, they’ve brought it on themselves, they’ve brought it on all of us. There’s a certain satisfaction in seeing the truth dawning. Look around—now who’s wise? Homo sapiens, we’re so wise, we’re so clever. Oh really, look around you and weep. Anyway, I braved it, I went down into the town for a nose round, I wanted to feel what it would be like after.'

'After what?'

'After they're gone. I wanted to feel the peace. I swam through the window of a house, and floated round the room on the back of a red sofa, my head high and swirling with happiness.'

'You might've drowned.'

'Not me, I once held the record for long-distance sewer swimming—anyway, I floated away from that house on a garden table, so carefree I didn't mind where it took me; eventually I washed up nicely at the bottom of Spring Hill but my peace was spoiled by seeing a trail of them heading up to the woods. They've made a camp up there and they're mucking up the place already.'

20

Future Vision

After a few days the waters dropped a little but the town was not safe. The sea that I had longed for was coming to me. The new, unfinished sea defences were all breached. Many could not return to their homes and a camp was growing in the woods. All types of people were levelled as they stood like trees, naked before the weather.

This concerned me. 'Won't they die in the woods?' I asked Charlie. 'I mean humans are tender, aren't they? Don't they die if left outdoors?' Surely no one would live in a house, away from all that was fresh and alive, unless they had no choice.

'People are sort of half-hardy,' said Charlie, 'for now.'

Eva did her bit and took in three lodgers.

Sperrin's ground floor had flooded: his fortress breached with no one in particular to blame. He wanted to blame the council but he himself had lobbied for the underground car parks, now useless, rather than the new sea defences. Some months after the flood a 'for sale' sign went up outside his house. Oona told Charlie that Sperrin pictured himself in a castle on some high ground where he could defend himself against the hungry and homeless, but houses on the coast could not be given away and all the castles were taken. Oona went to join the camp in the woods.

I watched the news and saw that things were just as bad all along the coast. In some places it was much worse. The government was putting up thousands of emergency homes on higher ground.

'This is just the beginning,' Wilfred said. 'Will you admit now that these critters have to be put down?'

'That's not how I would put it. Like I always say: in a garden you've got to get on with your neighbours. Maybe the humans will understand that now.'

'And if they don't?'

'The gardener comes along and digs them out.'

Together we felt the approach of wisdom. The Pica herself dropped down among my leaves.

'How does the work progress?' she asked.

'The gnosis does not spread much beyond the garden, except through seed,' I reported.

Her hooded head bowed up and down. 'Then we must ensure that the seeds of the garden are preserved throughout the catastrophes which lie ahead. This task has fallen to the boy, I believe.'

Wilfred looked a bit sniffy at this, but he kept quiet.

'The garden and the boy will begin the new co-operative. The humans must acknowledge their dependency and show due respect. If they fail, the balance of power is with the plant kingdom. Be open now,' she bade me, 'and receive your reward.'

Here was great knowledge: the forces and currents that muster and move the weather all around the planet were shown to me as one system. All was moody, turbulent and heaving. I was shown the sea of trees once more, and I was sickened to see that the Southern edge was rimmed with flames. I could only hope that things would heal with time.

The Pica read my mind and moved me forward to calmer times.

This is what I saw: a great glass dome in dry and utterly barren hills; inside full of life and greenery, vines climbing high into the roof, little enclosures with all kinds of animals penned there, a smell of hay, rustling and quiet munching. The animals, though, were a token presence next to the plants, which grew with a kind of stately grace and potency. They were the first of a new order.

Behind a glass screen I saw a man with astonished green eyes, like he never got over being born, now narrowed with purpose. He tapped data into a computer; a sparkling web crystallized on the screen. Before acting, the man was checking the effect of each change on the whole new ecosystem. 'Beneficial' flashed up. So he went on, inserting dormouse genes into the DNA of another animal. Dormancy would help the animal survive the harsh conditions it would have to face when released. Next, the man emptied some specks from a red matchbox labelled Ash, and then I was confident that my seeds were in good hands. My own fate didn't matter much to me as long as I knew that the seeds would carry on.

I heard a sound something between a sneeze and a hiccup. I saw Conal taking some food to a nest of big-eyed sweet-faced rodents; their enclosure was labelled 'gopi' and I knew that Charlie would find a way to save them too. Outside the dome was a ring of new green growth. Into this strip of life the green-eyed man released a cloud of insects.

Then from the shadows under the bench, where corn had spilled to the floor, another creature crept out and nibbled boldly at the grain, a creature with grey-brown fur and long yellow teeth: Wilfred, the great survivor.